EARL OF WESTON

ANNA ST. CLAIRE
WITH LAUREN HARRISON

Copyright © 2018 by Anna St. Claire
All rights reserved.

Cover Design by Teresa Spreckelmeyer
Edited by Heather King

This novel is entirely a work of fiction. The names, characters and incidents portrayed in it are the work of the author's imagination. Any resemblance to actual persons, living or dead, events or localities is entirely coincidental.

No part of this book may be reproduced in any form or by any electronic or mechanical means, including information storage and retrieval systems, without written permission from the author, except for the use of brief quotations in a book review.

This book is dedicated to any person who was once resigned to a life without love, until they met that special person who unpinned their world and sent it flying in a new, wonderful direction. This book is for you!

CHAPTER 1

LONDON 1816

*E*dward Hunter, Earl of Weston, leaned back in his chair and stretched, having shaken hands with his opponent, the Earl of Harrington. He was looking for relaxation, and feeling only slightly buoyed by his win.

Edward was one monkey richer after five games of piquet and feeling strangely discomfited. His friend wanted to play on, but he promised he could recoup his losses another time. Around the elegant gaming saloon at the private gentlemen's establishment known as The Wicked Earls' Club, various games of chance were in progress: roulette, vingt-et-un, faro, whist, and hazard. At the far end of the room, the billiards table sent a series of loud 'click clack' noises echoing now and then, above the general hum.

Edward fingered the small gold 'W' insignia on the pin anchoring his neck cloth. It was a modest emblem, but every member was required to wear his when in attendance. He had been presented with the pin eight months ago, following his induction into the club.

While the club was not in the most fashionable district, it compared favorably with White's on the richness of its interiors. The walls were papered in either deep burgundy or hunter green tones throughout, and the lighting was low. Only the most masculine furniture—rich leathers, dark wood grains—appointed the club's public rooms.

This was no genteel hell. Whilst exclusive, The Wicked Earls' Club was a disreputable establishment. Edward allowed his gaze to travel over the heads of the other earls present. Some were doing their best to run through their fortunes before the year was out; others were living outrageously on the expectancy to inherit. In varying stages of disarray, these sons of gentlemen were lounging in the plush leather armchairs, swilling expensive wine as though it was ale, and engaging in good-humored ribaldry.

The lamps were turned low, apart from those above the tables, but from his discreet corner, Edward could see the flushed faces and smell the aromas of excitement and stale cologne. Beside the grand fireplace, one gentleman was playing hazard with the Earl of St. Seville, who had a large pile of promissory notes at his right hand. The man's hair clung in damp fronds to his brow and his cheeks burned a florid tale. He was clearly being fleeced. It was not an uncommon occurrence, but for some reason Edward felt queasy and looked away. When had he become so easily affronted?

A blue haze of smoke wafted above the dark wood tables. Frederick, the Earl of Davenport, tilted his head back at that moment and added another long plume to the fog. Bright red splotches rode his cheekbones and his eyes held a wild expression that tobacco alone could not produce.

"Harrington," he called, as that earl approached the roulette table. "Care to try your luck against the bank?"

"Who holds the bank?" Harrington asked.

"I do."

"Then I must respectfully decline. You have the devil's own luck, Davenport."

Edward grinned. At least one of them was capable of exercising circumspection. Rising from his chair, he walked towards the door. An ear-splitting yelp, followed by booming laughter, caught his attention and he glanced back. Harrington had joined a lively game of hazard with the Earl of Grayson and some others. They appeared to be consoling Grayson on his losses in the time honoured manner—with ridicule and banter. Unrepentant, Edward smiled and left the room to head down the hall in the direction of the morning room. Distracted by his thoughts, he opened the door in front of him. Too late, he realized he had intruded upon a private party.

"Weston! Join us."

He started at hearing his name, and peered into a low-lit, smoke-filled room, unable to make out the identity of the gentleman who had called out to him.

"Come on in, Weston. We have an extra." Edward knew he should recognize the sandy-headed man who had just pulled back from his pipe, but he could not place him. The man pointed to a meagerly clothed, dark-haired woman. She smiled and invited him to join her, beckoning with her finger.

"Thank you, but no." Edward gave an ironic bow. "If you will excuse me, I have a friend meeting me shortly." He backed out of the room, closing the door behind him. Spotting the door he was looking for, he opened it and fairly flew down the stairs to the first floor. The whole scene upstairs struck him as distasteful, and the sudden realization confused him.

A footman appeared with a salver bearing a selection of decanters and glasses, and held open a door at the front end of the hall. Edward acknowledged the gesture. "You have perfect timing. Thank you."

"Yes, my lord." The servant's eyelids flickered but he gave no other sign of anything being untoward. Edward became conscious that a cloud of smoke had followed him and allowed the man a rueful nod. He sniffed his own coat jacket and smirked. His valet would likely burn it. This jacket had been a favorite; it was comfortable. But there were plenty of others to replace it.

"I will have a brandy if there is still some to be had," he said, dismissing the footman to attend to his request. He entered the morning room and discovered it was empty. A smell of rich cherry tobacco greeted him. The corner fireplace had a small fire burning in the grate and warmed the room. The space was welcoming and would provide a pleasant respite from his earlier activity.

Edward hated his current circumstances. Having returned from Paris and his latest commission for the Crown, he had been met with devastating news. His brother was dead from a bullet discharged during a duel, but not a bullet fired by either duelist. And then, his father had died within a fortnight of Edward's return. He had no aspirations to take his father's title; it was supposed to have passed to his brother. Yet now he had inherited the earldom. Earl of Weston was not a role he had been trained to handle. It had been thrust upon him. His life now was damnable. He had responsibilities he had neither wanted nor sought, and the occupation he loved—working for the Crown—had been pushed aside. He missed his brother, Robert, and wondered how things had deteriorated so much between them. They had been close most of their lives. He was slowly accepting his responsibility for the arguments over his recklessness and gambling, realizing that they created many of their problems. *This should have been Robert's club.*

Leaning back, he propped his legs on an ottoman, comfortable in the brown leather chair tucked in the corner of the room. The Club had become his refuge, and he could now understand the other gentlemen's attachment to it. After an afternoon of gambling, he was content to nurse another brandy, thankful for a darkness and the quiet the club offered in which to scan the news sheets. Edward scrutinized the date—even last week's issue would be better than none, since he had not read it yet. It was late, so most of the members had left for evening assignations, excepting the few who were still occupied in the private rooms. He opened the paper and shook out the folds, hoping to read it without interruption. A salacious story sometimes succeeded in removing his thoughts from the pernicious life he was leading.

After a few minutes, he recognized the booming voice of his best friend, Thomas Bergen, greeting Henry, the club doorman in the entrance hall. Moments later, Bergen sauntered through the doors.

"Care for some company?" Not waiting for an answer, Bergen sat down and waved over a footman. "I think I shall catch up with you, old friend." He nodded towards the glass in Edward's hand. "I have had an especially profitable time at the tables, and am in the mood to relax."

"Of course. How fortuitous! It seems that Lady Fortune was smiling at both of us this day. I picked up a monkey—playing piquet, no less." Edward recalled the vowels he carried in his pocket. *If only I could have quit when I was ahead before now, perhaps Robert would still be alive.* His pain was profound.

Edward looked into his friend's face. The man was every bit his equal, and lately, his opposite. His dark eyes were usually full of laughter and promised levity. Edward, however, had rarely been in the mood for humor these past months. His mother used to remark on the two—Bergen's and his own dark hair, both heads of the same height. They were easy to spot. Women found Bergen hard to ignore. Maybe that was the reason for his constant smiling state; or, Edward reflected, it could be his friend's affable nature, which attracted the women. No matter; as far as he was concerned, Bergen and his good disposition were not welcome—at least today.

"Of course. Do as you please." Edward casually pulled out his cigarro case and slid it across the table to Bergen. "Have one." He did not really want company, but it was rare when Thomas, the fifth Earl of Bergen, did not also appear at the Club at the same time Edward was there. They had been friends since childhood, and he'd been the one to give his friend the nickname of Thomas which had stuck all these years. Bergen was more of a brother to him than his own brother had been. He wondered why Robert kept invading his thoughts. A familiar sadness took root, and his attitude soured. *Fool that he was, he could not go an hour without thinking of his brother. Robert was there, a shadowy presence in every waking and sleeping moment.*

"What brings you here tonight, Bergen? As you might surmise from my being in this corner, I was looking for a little time alone." Edward's tone was brusque but he knew Thomas was given to ignoring his temper, normally responding to it with humor.

"I must be impervious to that black mood of yours, because I still enjoy your company. Perhaps a jug of vinegar would help your temperament more than the expensive brandy you are quaffing."

Bergen chuckled while swirling brandy in his own glass. "Has there been any word on Hampton? I thought I had heard he was back in Town."

"No, none." Edward felt the hair on the back of his neck prickle, and he sat forward in the chair. "Where did you get your information? I find it odd that I was not also told. I left word with Colonel Whitmore, at Headquarters, to let me know as soon as he was sighted. He assured me they would let me know."

"I heard his name mentioned at a gaming hell, earlier tonight. It is quite curious. How long has it been, Edward?" Bergen lowered his voice and studied his friend.

"It has been nine months, and I am no closer to an answer." Edward finished his drink and poured himself another.

"I stopped at Headquarters on my way here. They may have news for you. The murder of a peer is serious business." Bergen rolled the unlit cigarro between his lips. "Have you received any more details?"

"No, nothing as yet. I am still hoping Hampton can provide a clue; maybe he saw something. Perhaps there is a connection to his prolonged disappearance." Edward stared into his brandy. Guilt at not being here for his brother seeped into his head, and he fought to keep his thoughts to himself. It was useless with Bergen.

"I know you feel some responsibility for Robert's death. Edward, you know it is nonsense. You were not in Town. You had no way to know what would happen. You were not here to stop the duel. And if you had been here, who can say there would have been a different outcome?"

"Logical and perceptive as always, Thomas." His tone was sarcastic. "The reasonable part of me knows that, but my heart will not accept it. Had I been here, I would have been Robert's second—providing I could not talk him out of such a foolish start."

"Believe it or not, I understand." Bergen's voice was compassionate.

The door from the back hallway flew open, hitting the wall with a crash. Several men, most likely emerging from the private rooms, were probably heading for new pursuits. Gaudily dressed women hung on the gentlemen's arms, displaying their wares with abandon. One woman wore a low-cut lace dress that barely covered her bosom; the other wore a bright yellow gown with black trimming which appeared to belong to someone a size or two smaller. Bright red lipstick and spots of heavy rouge drew attention to artificial faces. Perfumes of floral and fruit scents battled for distinction. Two more such women trailed behind the men, without partners. These were not the type of lady of whom his mother would approve.

One of the jades looked his way, and Edward realized too late that his brief glance had given her the wrong idea.

"My lord." A buxom blonde, with startling, bright red lips, tottered his way, and sat on his lap. She was definitely not from his mother's circle, he thought, grinning.

"See something to amuse you, do you, handsome?" She boldly touched his face and allowed the tip of her tongue to peep between her teeth.

Edward felt her fingers slowly drifting across his cheek, coming to rest on his lips. Her seductive message was hard to mistake, particularly when she rocked her hips in a movement as old as time.

Bergen smirked, and raised his glass. "Shall I give you some privacy?"

"No!" His voice elevated, Edward shot his friend a quelling glare. "That will not be necessary."

"What do you say I work the knots out of your shoulders, my lord?" She placed her hands on either side of his neck and rubbed deeply with her thumbs. "Hmm...is that pleasing to you, my lord?"

The woman winked at him, and smiled, showing red lip pomade carelessly smeared on her front teeth. She had obviously been employing her charms in one of the private backrooms. The thought repulsed him. "Madame, while I kindly appreciate your generous offer, I am not in the mood for any...entertainment." He moved her off his lap, and abruptly stood her on her feet. Digging into his pocket, he grabbed a gold coin and tossed it her way. "My friend and I were having a private discussion." He scowled, no longer amused. He had no interest in what she had to sell.

Miffed, she snatched up the coin and left, brushing off her red skirt as she rushed past him. Holding the handle of the door, she looked back.

"You could have used a good tumble, my lord," she said, her tone acetic. A moment later, he heard Henry call for the footman to usher them to the back door. His voice was a little more forceful than his usual tone. He had been surprised they were allowed in the morning room, and was glad to hear Henry send them out the backdoor.

Bergen whistled. "Losing your touch, are you, Edward? Making the ladies angry is not going to ease your needs." He sipped his drink and smiled.

"Have you anything important to tell me? If not, I have readied her for you." He rustled his paper, hoping his friend would take it as a sign he wanted to be alone.

Bergen chuckled. "Yes, as a matter of fact, I do have business with you. You know you cannot be rid of me so easily, Weston."

"I am all astonishment!" He did not really want his friend to leave and was glad he could not chase him off. "Damn! I am in worse shape than I thought. She did nothing for me." He looked at his lap, now disgusted with himself. "Maybe her amusement would have been just the thing." His body, however, told him otherwise.

"Along with the pox?" Bergen laughed, and then abruptly cleared his throat. "On a more serious note, I have a note for you." Reaching into his pocket, he pulled out a sealed letter and handed it to Edward.

"Coventry asked me to pass it on to you while I was at Head-quarters."

Weston,

Hampton in town, and has been invited to the Bentley house party starting on Friday. Has an interest in Lady Pennywaite. Invitations for you and Bergen are waiting at your homes. The visit could prove useful to your search. Acceptance already sent on both yours and Bergen's behalf. Make plans to attend.

Coventry

Edward wadded the note up and tossed it into the fire. "It seems I am going to a house party, my friend. I do not know the size of the affair, but it appears I need to go."

"It would appear we are both going. The man knows everything." Bergen grinned again. "Surely there will be card games, wagers, and ladies? This is the type of work I always enjoy. I suppose the invitations will give details of the location, but I believe the Bentley family is at their country estate. I will ride over in the morning and we can leave together, my friend."

～

"Are you ready, Miss Longbottom?" the curate asked when he arrived to drive Hattie to the posting house to catch the stage.

"Bottom! Bottom!" Archie mimicked proudly. The curate's cheeks at once turned red.

"I suppose I am as ready as I can be," Hattie replied miserably, barely noticing her parrot's effrontery in the midst of her own distress.

"Little Whitley Parish will miss having you here," he replied while lifting her trunk and warily eyeing the large, exotic, green bird.

"I have never known anywhere else, but it was bound to happen sooner or later. Mrs. Bromley will take care of the flowers for the church, and will organize the sewing for the parish poor. Miss Gates will play the organ," she prattled on as they stood in the empty entrance hall.

"Your loss will be felt acutely," he said kindly. "For many years your family has been selfless servants to our parish."

"No one will know I am gone, before long," she said, dabbing at her eyes and blowing her nose with her handkerchief.

She pushed her spectacles farther up her nose and looked around. The house was empty and, she reflected with a pang of sadness, ready for the next occupants. It had not been a bad life, precisely, but very, very dull. Dull suited her admirably.

"I suppose there is no use in putting it off any longer. Come, Archie." Hattie held open the cage and the parrot obediently flew inside. She closed the front door behind her for the last time and walked out to the pony cart, feeling as though she was facing her doom.

The curate signaled the chestnut mare to move forward and she held onto Archie's cage with one hand and her bonnet with the other, as the cart lurched forward.

Harriet Eleanor Longbottom was a spinster. There was no other way to describe herself. She had given up her bloom to be a companion to her ailing mother, who by sly hints or subtle looks had convinced Hattie that she was indispensable to her health. Look at where it had left her, Hattie thought morosely. Somehow, six and twenty years had passed and not once had she left Worcestershire.

She had been faced with two choices when her mother died, and was grateful to have been permitted any opinion on the matter, for many were not so fortunate. She could live with her aunt, who had forbidden her to bring her beloved companion, Archie, or remove to Oxfordshire to her brother's estate and play aunt to his brood of five. There was really no choice.

Now, as she sat on the stage, crowded between two very large and disagreeable men, she was having second thoughts. One was a lecher, Hattie was convinced, for he sat as close as possible and was touching her leg on purpose! The other had never seen a bar of soap, she was certain, and her sense of smell would surely never be the same again.

It had been a very close thing to even be allowed on the stage with Archie. She had been obliged to pay an exorbitant bribe to the driver and still she had to hold the cage in her lap!

Across from her, a female of loose morals was displaying, in addition to heavily rouged cheeks, an overabundance of bosom overflowing from her scandalously low-cut scarlet gown. Hattie could not even look her in the eye, she was so ashamed as the woman flirted and exposed her ankles to the lecher.

The driver was moving at a frightful pace, and the conveyance tipped sideways around every bend in the road. Hattie prayed for all of their souls as steadfastly as she could, or sang hymns to Archie when he grew loud. He did have an unfortunate tendency to repeat words he heard or shriek when he was excited. She had never before considered she might be forced to travel on the stage with him.

When they stopped in Wolverstone for a change of horses, Hattie was most grateful for a chance to stretch her legs and breathe the fresh air. As she alighted precariously, her legs stiff, while at the same time balancing Archie's cage on her hip, a pair of riders flew by them, splashing mud all over the passengers and causing Hattie nearly to drop her bird.

Strings of oaths and curses were bellowed at the riders by driver and passenger alike, many of them words Hattie's pure ears had never before heard.

"Shite! Jackass!" Archie mimicked to roars of laughter. The sounds echoed around them.

"Mind your tongue!" she scolded Archie in horror, shaking her head as she did so. Her spectacles flew off and she heard the ominous sound of glass crushing.

"Drat!" she muttered, and fell to her knees to search for her faculty of sight. She was quite blind beyond five feet without them.

While the other passengers hurried inside to take advantage of the chance to refresh themselves, Hattie continued to search on the ground.

"Are you looking for these?" a deep, aristocratic voice asked. Dimly, Hattie perceived what remained of her spectacles as he held them out to her.

Something about the man's voice gave her pause and she did not want to look up at him. He was close enough that she could see his gleaming Hessians, and knew he was Quality. Suddenly self-conscious, she wanted to tidy herself before she stood up, but his hand was reaching down to assist her. His hands were large and elegant, even in his leather riding gloves, and they were strong enough to lift her lightly to her feet without apparent effort.

ANNA ST. CLAIRE & WITH LAUREN HARRISON

"Thank you, sir," she said with a slight tremble in her voice, still too shy to make eye contact, though she could make out most of his features from under her lashes.

The tall, dark stranger inclined his head and walked into the inn with his companion who had waited nearby, watching.

Hattie squinted after them, yet could see nothing but blurry movement.

Suddenly, she felt a pinch to her bottom and squealed in outrage. She turned to see the lascivious passenger; he was evidently amused by his antics as his large belly rumbled and his multiple chins quivered with laughter.

"How dare you!" she screeched with indignation.

"How dare you! How dare you!" Archie mimicked.

The driver blew the warning horn. She had not even managed five feet past the coach. How could it already be time to leave again?

"Driver!" She raised her voice, trying to get to his attention. "This man assaulted me and I refuse to ride inside with him!"

"She must be mistaken," the man said, feigning innocence. "Why would I want to touch her?" He sneered.

"Sorry, miss. Are there any witnesses?" the driver asked impatiently.

The other passengers shook their heads.

"Then we must be going. 'Tis your word against his."

Hattie watched as everyone climbed into the coach.

"I refuse to ride with this man. Sir, I must insist!"

"As you wish, miss." The guard slammed the coach door shut and hopped on the back as the driver gathered up the reins with a flick of the whip. The horses took off, splattering mud in her face. Spitting the excess earth from her mouth, she stared after the vehicle in disbelief, the distance growing rapidly as it sped away from her. What had just happened? Was there no goodness left in this world outside Little Whitley?

Hattie stood there for a full five minutes before she realized the implications of what had happened. She was stranded in a strange town without her belongings, except for a bird and her reticule.

Turning to face the inn, she picked up the cage and went inside.

The shabby inn was bustling with custom on this busy coaching road. Never before had she seen so many strangers. It smelled of smoke, sweat, and ale. She swallowed hard so she would not give in to her anger or her fright. Clearing her throat, she addressed the man she hoped to be the innkeeper since he seemed to be giving directions to the serving maids. It was her first time in such an establishment, and she had little idea how to proceed.

"Sir, could you please tell me when the next stage is due? The one I arrived on has left without me."

"Not until tomorrow, the same time," he grunted, looking at her with disapproval. She glanced down at herself; she had some splatters of mud, but certainly not outrageous in her blacks. Then she realized it was Archie he was staring at, an expression of considerable wariness shaping his features.

"What is your destination, miss?"

"I was to take this stage to Eynsham and my brother is to meet me there."

"It is only another few miles. Do you ride? I have horses for hire."

"I am afraid not," she replied.

"The gentlemen in the parlor are heading west, I think I heard them say."

"We are not acquainted," she said, bristling with affront. As if a single lady could ask a gentleman she did not know for anything, she wanted to point out.

"They have probably ridden here, anyway. You could walk," he suggested, clearly running out of patience.

She stared at the man in horror. She had spent six hours traveling in the most uncomfortable conditions, had been assaulted, and now her worldly possessions were lost.

"I must attend to the other customers. You may use the parlor, there are only the two gentlemen in there. He pointed to a door across the common room before he walked away. She watched him go, flustered and frustrated that she had no one to help her.

Hattie made her way as best she could through the blur to where she thought the parlor was. When she entered, she could not believe her eyes. Was she imagining things? She squinted.

No, there was indeed a barmaid sitting atop the knees of one of the gentlemen—and her chest was falling out of her bodice.

"I have walked into the devil's lair!" Hattie shrieked. Imagining the worst, she covered her eyes. She could see enough to know it was the gentleman and his friend from earlier, as the only thing she dared look at was his boots.

"Bugger, she's crazed." The second man laughed as the barmaid tried to tidy herself.

"Bugger! Bugger! Bugger!" Archie crowed unhelpfully, sensing his mistress's distress.

"Madam, cease your vapors at once!" one of the men commanded. "It is not at all what you think."

"I do not want to know, you imp of Satan! I know all about gentlemen such as yourself—whoremongers and, and rogues! Reverend Hastings reminds me every Sunday." She struggled to think of harsh enough names to call them.

"I am certain he does," the man said dryly.

Hattie's cheeks began to heat as she noticed the man looking her over like a piece of beefsteak. He was entirely too close for her comfort. Oh, no, he would not find her willing as the serving wench. She took Archie and ran for the door as fast as her feet would go. Five miles suddenly did not seem so far to walk.

CHAPTER 2

Edward and Bergen finished their lunch of mutton pie and ale, content to have had time to rest whilst the ostlers rubbed down and fed their horses.

"I do not know when I have enjoyed lunch more. I have not laughed so much in an age." Bergen mounted his large black gelding and the two men set off for Eynsham. "I fear your touch with the females continues, my friend. I must say, though, we picked the best place to stop. Where else might we have gotten such delightful entertainment?"

"I agree, my friend! I was trying to decide whether the circus was also staying at the inn." Edward laughed at the memory. "That young lady and her screaming bird…it did indeed feel good to laugh."

"You imp of Satan! Imp, imp, imp," Bergen mimicked.

The intonation was a perfect mimic of the bird. Edward could not help but chuckle, which sent them off hooting with laughter, until a piercing shriek startled the horses.

"It came from around the bend, just ahead." Edward pulled back on the reins, steadying his mare as she sidled and attempted to swing round.

"Easy, girl." He patted her sleek neck.

ANNA ST. CLAIRE & WITH LAUREN HARRISON

"Bugger. Whoremongers! Bugger. Whoremongers!"

"Could it be?" Bergen chortled, his dark hair wild from the ride.

"After you, my friend. There is only one way to find out."

The two men nudged their horses forward. As they rounded the bend in the narrow, tree-lined road, they spotted the woman from the inn, doggedly walking, carrying her bird cage propped on her right hip.

"Were you not recently at the Roaring Lion Inn?" Edward could not resist enquiring.

The unprepossessing female looked up and squinted at them, her upper lip almost touching her nose from the effort, but said nothing. Instead, she kept walking.

"Bugger! Whoremongers!" the bird crowed the words.

"Archie, please be quiet." The woman tapped the cage with her free hand.

"Archie? His name is Archie?" Bergen's tone was teasing.

"Yes, do you find that amusing, my lord? I confess that I am at a loss as to why the name Archie would be humorous to you. He is my long-time companion, and a wonderful friend," she replied defensively.

Edward cleared his throat. "Mayhap we can be of assistance, my lady." Somewhat belatedly, he had realized that her polished accents, as well as her clothing, even as mud-stained as they were, were Quality. Her dull brown hair hung in disarray about her pale cheeks, and he was reminded that her hair had been in a severe chignon when he last saw her. The loose hair softened her appearance considerably, he noticed.

"Whoremongers!" Archie filled in the silence.

"Archie! Please, hush." The woman's face blazed with embarrassment. "I fear I must apologize for his chatter. He is nervous."

"May we inquire your destination, miss?" Bergen offered. "This would not be the best road for a lady to be traveling..." His throat worked. "...with a parrot."

"I have had an abominable day already, thank you," she answered tartly. "I hope you are enjoying yourself at my expense, my lord. For your information, I was abandoned by the stage-coach, which left with all of my belongings except for Archie. I did not get a chance to eat, either, due to..." She broke off with a cough. "Well, you know what prevented me from doing so." The lady continued walking without turning to look at either rider.

Edward stayed quiet, considering. They certainly could not allow her to walk along this road. Highwaymen were known to frequent this road, aided by the thick trees and brush that flanked both sides of the road for long stretches at a time.

"Perhaps we could start by introducing ourselves, since we lack some acquaintance to perform this office." He hoped this would not be a mistake he would regret. "My name is Weston," he said, "and this is Lord Bergen." Signaling to his friend, he stopped his horse and dismounted. Bergen followed his lead and they began to walk alongside the lady and her outlandish bird.

He waited for her to introduce herself.

Begrudgingly she replied, "Miss Longbottom."

Clearing his throat—Edward assumed to prevent further ill-timed and riotous laughter—Bergen joined in, perhaps also realizing this woman needed help. "Miss, might we inquire where you are going?"

"My lords, I assure you, I am quite...splendid." She puffed the last word, clearly tiring from the exertion of carrying the parrot and his cage.

"My lady, would you care to share the nature of your destination? Lord Bergen and I would be happy to be of assistance. In good conscience, we cannot ride on and leave a lady alone in such circumstances, even with a...companion."

"We are appointed to meet with my brother. He will surely be looking for my arrival this afternoon. I am to meet him in Eynsham, at the post-house."

Edward looked at Bergen. "Miss Longbottom, we, too, are journeying west and Eynsham is but a few miles along our route. As we are travelling in the same direction, I propose that we dispense with niceties and turn to more practical matters. The weather is chilly, with intermittent periods of cold rain, and you appear to be—quite understandably—tired." He stopped and took a breath, unsure he really wanted to do what he was about to do. "My lady, can you ride?"

Miss Longbottom squinted at them. "Sir, I do not," she replied in a most precise tone. "What are you suggesting?"

"That we take you up with us, miss. We assure you, we are honorable in our intentions, and only wish to deliver you safely to your destination so you may meet your brother." Edward half hoped she would decline and he could continue his journey, knowing he had been a gentleman.

Miss Longbottom looked around, peering first at her surroundings and then up at the strangers. "I cannot handle a horse, my lord."

"Of course. But I was proposing you merely ride. I will handle the horse. You can ride with me. I know this is not what you would wish, but I am a gentleman, and you are a lady in need of…" He struggled for the right word. He did not want to laugh. "In need of assistance," he concluded after a moment.

Bergen offered his help. "I will be much obliged to carry your… Archie." He bit his lip and kept a straight face, although Edward could see the effort it took.

"Well, I do not know what to say." She looked down at her mud-stained boots, and then at her bird.

"Obliged to help! Whoremongers!" Archie shrieked, repeating Edward's words of a moment ago.

The two men looked at each other and grinned. This could be one of the more interesting trips he had taken, Edward mused, watching the parrot prattling on with his new favorite phrase.

"It seems that Archie is game," Edward suggested, allowing a grin to spread across his face.

"Archie is not terrified of horses and has his own cage," she countered.

She bit her lip, a determined look to her face. Edward could see she was struggling with the decision.

"You promise me that I will be safe in the saddle with you? I have not forgotten those wicked scenes in the parlor."

"I assure you, Athena is a gentle mare." He would make sure of it.

"And yourself?" She looked up at him bravely, and at last he could see her eyes. They were an ocean-blue and mesmerizing.

"My lady, as I said earlier, it was not as it seemed. The serving wench dropped a bowl of hot soup over her dress and we were attempting to help blot up the hot liquid before she scalded herself." Edward returned wryly.

"Sir, her *bosoms* were on display," she bit out, her cheeks bright red from having said such a word.

Tedious, righteous virgins, Edward thought in disgust. Why were they bothering? He wanted to stop this ridiculous display of chivalry and let the silly chit keep walking with her bird... but his upbringing would not allow him.

"Her...chest...was exposed because she fell out of her dress. It was a most inopportune moment you witnessed, I assure you. We are *innocent* of any wrong-doing." Edward made a careful, measured response.

"Innocent! Bosoms!" Archie squawked, his feathers flapping.

Edward quirked a brow at the intrusive bird, and drew in a deep breath. He sensed his irritation was showing.

"Miss Longbottom, I am not going to argue with you or your bird any further, and neither will we leave you on this road. You are safe, and you are coming with us." Before she could utter another word, Edward lifted her up onto his saddle, and mounted his grey mare, settling in behind his prudish passenger. His mare nodded her head, but made no objections to the added burden.

Bergen took the cage from her fist. He mounted his steed, with Archie and cage in hand. His horse objected to carrying the bulky cage as side baggage, snorting and tossing his head.

The woman was blissfully silent. He was grateful for the awkward peacefulness. Edward noticed her knuckles were white from gripping the pommel of his saddle and she was leaning as far forward as she could. *Priggish, ridiculous female!* She might be attractive if she were not always squinting and forcing her lip to roll up into her nose in an effort to see. He recalled her broken glasses and sighed. *Thankfully, this good deed would not take long, and they could be on their way,* he thought, nudging Athena into a canter.

Hattie had always been terrified of horses, and was horrified at the thought of riding on such a large animal, but her feet already ached from Archie's extra weight and she had not yet walked above a mile. By now, her brother, Richard, would be wondering where she had got to. It was a lowering realization that her morals were so fickle, she could sink to such depths in one day as to ride with these gentlemen of ill repute. She dared not think all of her mother's and the Reverend's warnings about the heathen world out there!

"I am considered an expert horseman, miss," Weston stated. He was staring at her expectantly, she noticed, squinting. It was then she realized he was waiting to boost her up. She lifted her foot, expecting him to provide a lift with his interlocked fingers but instead, he placed his hands on her waist and she was thrust upon the horse as though she were as light as one of Archie's feathers. She could still feel the warmth from his hands on her waist and she tittered with near hysteria. When he mounted up behind her, and she could feel his thighs against hers and his chest against her back, she knew she would soon die of mortification.

"Oh fudge," she muttered.

"Oh fudge! Whoremongers!" Archie repeated. He began to make a raucous, screeching sound.

"Hush!" she reprimanded, beginning to feel vaporish.

"Does your bird repeat everything he hears?"

"Not always, no. Only when he is anxious or excited."

Weston's arm came around her and she leaned forward to place some distance between their two bodies. She was trembling from fear and she tried not to look down.

"What is your direction?" he asked casually as they rode at a mild cantor along the hedge-lined road.

"I am to live with my brother. My mother passed away recently and he has graciously offered me a home with his family."

"Please accept my condolences. I should have apprehended such an occurrence by your mourning attire."

"Thank you, sir. She was an invalid for the past decade. I have scarcely left her side since I was six and ten."

"Your mother was fortunate to have such a devoted daughter."

Hattie harrumphed. "She would not have had it any other way, sir."

Weston made a sound as though he were smothering a laugh. She turned to discover how Archie was faring but could only see his green body bobbing up and down on the horse. She could not make out the other gentleman's face with any clarity.

"And you, sir, where are you bound?" She politely returned the query.

"An insipid house party, I am afraid. Duty calls."

They rounded a curve in the road rather briskly and she held onto the pommel and mane with all her might. She was certain she was splayed ungracefully across the poor horse's neck.

Weston slowed the horse once they had straightened again, but she was still afraid to open her eyes or let go of the mane.

A gentle hand was trying to tug her upright.

"By Jove, is that Livingston ahead?" Bergen called. Hattie could see nothing but a blur of black.

"I think it is," Weston replied.

"I'll wager you a monkey we can overtake him before Eynsham."

Where they speaking of a race? Hattie wanted no part of this. She was finally beginning to settle and feel perhaps there was some gentlemanly behavior to be found in this pair. Then she was pulled back into his chest.

"What are you doing?" she shrieked.

"Hold on my dear, this will not take a minute," he whispered in her ear, holding her body plastered up against him in a most vulgar fashion which sent strange new sensations coursing through her stomach.

Soon they were galloping so hard her entire body was jarred and clods of mud flew everywhere. If she was not blind before, then she was sure to be now. Her bonnet came untied and she could feel the wind whipping her hair. It would be exhilarating if she did not fear she would fall to her death.

"I demand you to stop at once!" She squinted up at him, until a whiff of dust found her nose. She fought to hold back the sneeze threatening.

"Sorry, my love. It will be over in a moment." His voice was dripping with amusement.

She attempted to wriggle free, fearing she would be safer on the ground.

"Be still, woman!" he shouted at her as he pulled on the reins and slowed.

"You, sir, are no gentleman! Racing with a gently bred lady on your horse surpasses...everything!" she exclaimed, trying to catch her breath, which was heaving violently in her chest.

The two gave each other at look, but she could not make it out. The men dismounted, and Weston assisted her down from Athena. Bergen handed Archie to her. They both bowed regally.

"I humbly beg your pardon, miss," Weston said, but she could not determine if he was mocking her or not.

"Are you certain this is your destination?" he asked.

"Yes, quite. This is where Richard was to meet me, but I would not go one foot further with either of you blackguards!"

"Very well. Good day to you, miss. Good day to you, Archie," Weston said pleasantly.

"Good day! Bosoms! Whoremongers!" Archie returned to the bellowing laughter of the two gentlemen. Hattie watched them gracefully remount and raise their hats as they rode away, as though they had done her a great favor.

CHAPTER 3

The two riders turned off the main road onto a pebbled drive, heavily lined with oak trees, just as the weather turned wet. Edward noticed that the trees protected them from the light drizzle.

Bergen broke the silence with a snigger. "I say, Livingston was startled to see me pull ahead of him, carrying a bird cage and parrot, no less. He is probably still laughing. But you and Miss Longbottom had already bested him—the woman was practically glued to you."

"He seemed equally entertained with Miss Longbottom. Especially when she started reciting Bible verses as soon as we stopped. Interesting spinster, I think. Gaining a monkey was worth the brief discomfort. I was thoroughly diverted!"

Edward's horse suddenly nodded and neighed, as if in response, causing both men to hoot with laughter.

The trees thinned as a three-story brick home came into view. "It has been a long time since I have been here. I believe the last was some sort of affair for Coventry, and it was a tedious bore. As I recall, I thought Lord and Lady Brentley were the most ill-suited couple. She was loud and wearing, and he was affable and undemanding." He was silent for a moment. "Bizarre as it is, I cannot stop thinking of that mad parrot and the righteous spinster." Edward chuckled at his new names for the odd pair. "He has more personality than his owner, I fear." It had been a long time since he had seen an exotic talking bird. The last time was an exhibit at a local fair, years ago.

"The impulse to race Livingston in company with the spinster and her bird was probably ill-advised on our part, although thoroughly entertaining. I thought your lady passenger would have an apoplexy. If you could have seen her face!" Bergen slapped his thigh with mirth. "I almost dropped the damn parrot!"

"I confess, I was not sure how we were going to make it the few miles we did." Edward did not wish to think about the imprudent race, nor the shockingly luscious body he had felt pressed up against him every step of the way. "Do you think this party will be well-attended? If I have to dance with wallflowers, I prefer at least to have a choice among them."

"Dance with wallflowers! Whoremongers!" Bergen mimicked Archie, chuckling at his own jest as they pulled up before the house. Jumping down, they both handed the reins to a waiting groom and simultaneously took the steps by two. It appeared Bergen was as anxious to get through the necessary formalities and relax in his room as Edward was.

"Thank goodness we are rid of that annoying pair, although I do not think I have had such fun in a while. I'm looking forward to a tumbler of good brandy and a bath. She was meeting her brother. Do you think he has a pet monkey?" They both laughed at the jibe, as they walked towards the door. *I need to focus on Hampton, not that pesky pair.* Despite the jokes at her expense, Edward found himself thinking of her.

A stooped and greying butler admitted them, and after taking their damp outer cloaks, ordered the footman to escort them to their bedchambers.

Lady Bentley greeted them on her way out of the house. "My lords! I was so happy to receive your acceptances. It is so good of you to come. You must be worn-out from your journey. Please allow our staff to address any requests you have." She hesitated, and then nodded towards the footman who stood ready to take the luggage.

"I sensed that she had much more to say," Bergen whispered.

"Be grateful she was headed out," he muttered. "I hope to find Hampton as soon as possible. His disappearance puzzles me." Edward spoke quietly as they headed upstairs to their rooms. "Mother still blames me for Robert's death, you know. To be honest, I cannot help but feel guilty because I was not here to help him—I knew Robert's betrothed was having an affair with Remington, and I chose to ignore it, irritated by his overbearing manner towards me. He chose Hampton as his second—and they had been friends since being in leading-strings. I find it hard to understand his disappearance, though. Instinct tells me he saw something, even if *he* does not realize it. When I approached his brother, Perry, he was insistent Hampton knew nothing...and I had only asked if Hampton was at home."

"That is curious."

"Yes, I found the defensiveness peculiar, in itself."

The footman stopped in front of two doors at the end of the hall. "My lords, these are your apartments. Please let me know if you require anything.

"We are next to each other."

"So, it appears. Do try to keep your liaisons to a dull roar," Bergen jested.

"If you will keep your snoring to one," Edward retorted.

"At least Archie will not be our neighbor tonight."

"Indeed." They laughed as they entered their respective chambers.

Edward opened his door, and the footman brought in his portmanteau, placing it on a stool next to the wash-hand stand. He noticed two comfortable brown leather chairs, already warming from facing the crackling fire in front of them.

"Ahem, would you bring me a decanter of brandy and a bath?" He issued his request just before the footman closed the door, causing the man to stop and turn.

"Yes, my lord. At once."

Edward pulled a cigarillo from his jacket, and using the fire, he lit it and settled back into one of the leather chairs. *It is curious indeed. I had not even considered the possibility of...*

A knock on his door stirred him from his contemplation. "Come in."

"My lord, your brandy." The footman entered, carrying a tray with a decanter and two glasses, placing them on the small table nestled between the two chairs.

"Thank you," Edward nodded and reached for the bottle. He uncorked it and poured himself a drink.

"Your bath is also here, my lord." The footman stepped aside as servants entered, carrying pails of water for the copper tub. They filled the tub and left the room.

Edward decided to just move the small table and decanter closer to the tub.

He swirled the amber liquid slowly before raising it to his lips and swigging it down. *That was precisely what I needed.* He refilled his glass and settled into his bath, his thoughts on the conversation with Hampton's brother. He had not given that exchange enough thought. Perry was very abrupt, which was out of character for him. He could not imagine what had got into him. Now that he thought more on this, though, what did Perry know? His behavior would suggest he knew something. Edward made a mental note to visit the man as soon as he returned to town. He then tossed down his drink and helped himself to a third from the nearby table, reasoning that it would help him to relax from the long ride while he bathed.

Two hours later, Edward knocked on Bergen's door.

Bergen opened it, still fastening his cuffs. "I almost overslept. I found the bath and nap very restorative. How about you, Weston?"

"Yes, I feel much better. Bentley's cellars are superb, particularly the brandy."

"I will have to sample that delightful beverage, perhaps after tonight's festivities."

The two men proceeded downstairs to join other guests who were gathering in the drawing room for tea. Edward quickly considered those guests already gathered. He caught sight of Lady Pennywaite, but not Hampton. Her ladyship appeared engaged in a rather flirtatious conversation with Lord Purdy. Edward nudged Bergen and discreetly nodded in her direction.

"What do you make of that?"

"Judging from her level of interest, I would say that Lord Hampton has not yet gained an advantage." He smirked and pointed to the door. Hampton had just entered and was heading in Lady Pennywaite's direction, a look of annoyance on his face.

"Ah. I was going to interrupt the two, but this could be an enjoyable interlude in what promises to be a boring evening." Edward accepted a glass of champagne as a footman passed them, and observed the trio. Lady Pennywaite stepped to the side, a look of feigned confusion on her face, as Lord Hampton and Lord Purdy began exchanging words. With the level of tension in the room, he could not hear them, so he began moving in their direction. A screech stopped him in his tracks.

Loud squawks erupted again from entrance hall.

"Bergen, tell me you did not hear what I just heard."

"It depends. If you are referring to the argument in front of us, I did not. But if you are referring to the too-familiar squawking coming from the doorway, I am afraid I did."

Both men exchanged their empty glasses for ones filled with champagne from the circulating footman and moved towards the hall doorway to observe discreetly from the threshold.

"I cannot believe this. What are they doing here?" Edward leered at the scene in front of them.

"Ah! I believe this house must belong to the brother and his wife. How delightful for us to be able to join our new friends again." Bergen grinned.

The two men watched the discourse between their hostess and her newest guests. Lady Louisa Bentley was speaking in harsh tones to Miss Longbottom. A familiar face squinted back at her hostess, gripping the cage with the screaming green parrot at her side. *So, this is her brother's home*, Edward mused. How had he missed the resemblance to Lord Bentley? Her brother never wore spectacles in public and both squinted in a similar fashion. He suspected Archie's outburst had little to do with Lady Bentley's rudeness and more to do with some hidden motive. Miss Longbottom looked crestfallen.

Lady Bentley made angry gestures towards her and then turned and moved in the direction he was standing. She stopped when she saw a footman and waved him to her side.

"Take her to the third floor, and place them in the furthest room in the maids' quarters," she ordered in a nasty tone. "It is empty and I wish to see her and her surly bird as little as possible while my guests are here." Her feelings towards the lady and Archie were abundantly clear. It infuriated him to see Miss Longbottom treated thus.

When had he become protective of her? Perhaps it was just that he was annoyed about the way she was being treated, although he could feel his temple pulsing with anger. He raised his hand and rubbed it. There might even be a small sense of guilt over her perceived humiliation earlier.

"Excuse me, my lady." He caught Lady Bentley's attention. "I could not help but overhear that you are unfortunately short of rooms. Miss Longbottom is a fond acquaintance of both Lord Bergen and myself. I will gladly offer my bedchamber for her use. I have but to collect my bag and I can then share Lord Bergen's accommodation."

"Nonsense. There will be no need for that. My wife has merely forgotten about the three new rooms we have had refurbished in anticipation of our guests." Lord Richard Bentley stepped into the hall and handed his cloak and cane to the waiting footman. "Louisa, please have the staff prepare a bath for my sister. She will certainly appreciate a brief respite before our festivities this evening." He smiled towards Weston and Bergen, but the glare of anger towards his wife was unmistakable. "Williams, take my sister's belongings to the pink velvet room and ask Sally to attend her."

"As you wish, my lord."

"And please take her companion, Archie, to the room as well." He turned to his wife and spoke in a low voice, away from the others. "They will not be dismissed to the third floor."

Lady Bentley flushed at the barely veiled reprimand.

"Yes, my lord." The footman led Miss Longbottom and Archie upstairs.

When his sister was out of view, Lord Bentley turned to his wife. "My dear, I believe we have everything in order. Let us join the others in the drawing room." He held out his arm for his wife to accompany him.

She turned to Edward. "My lord, you are so gallant. I do apologize for putting you in such a position. I am ashamed to say I had momentarily forgotten that extra rooms have already been prepared. I had planned to move my dear sister to a freshly appointed room tomorrow." She simpered. "How did you say that you became acquainted with my…husband's dearest sister?"

Smiling tightly, Edward forced a pleasant response. "I do not believe I did." He nodded and exchanged his empty glass for another filled one. "May we join you in the drawing room?" He and Bergen accompanied their host and hostess as they joined the rest of the guests.

Hattie sat on the edge of a chair after releasing Archie from his cage. She was miserable and exhausted—much too fatigued to give a fig for the fine room with its pink velvet draperies and matching rose wallpaper. A bath of water sat steaming in the corner of the room, calling her name. She was too tired to even consider the evening's festivities. No doubt, if he knew, the Reverend Hastings would accuse her of melodrama, but it had been the worst day of her life, and now Richard's wife hated her. Hattie would much rather stay in the attic than feel the ire of that Jezebel. How misguided in her had she been! Aunt Matilda's offer was looking more palatable—were it not for poor Archie.

If only Hattie had known Richard was hosting a house party, she would have delayed her arrival. Could this day get any worse? She needed a long, hot soaking bath and a good sleep. Perhaps she would

ANNA ST. CLAIRE & WITH LAUREN HARRISON

be able to laugh about the day's adventures some time, far-off in the future.

Pulling off her half-boots was almost too taxing, Hattie was so exhausted. However, such habits were well ingrained and she pulled her dirty dress over her head and began to rinse some of the day's traveling dust away, as she lowered herself into the readied bath.

Her gown was also in need of a thorough scrubbing—sponging would not do. Hattie had nothing but her petticoats and shift, with all her belongings having gone with the stage. She bit her lip in an effort not to give in to the doldrums. When she thought about the horrors of the day, she shuddered. It could have been worse; her person had not been irreparably harmed, only her dignity and her spectacles.

"Everything will appear better in the morning, Archie."

The parrot cocked his head to the side when she spoke to him and then bobbed his head up and down in agreement. Why could he not to be so agreeable when they were with strangers? Those two rogues who pretended to be gentlemen had encouraged Archie to misbehave!

Her temper flared and she scrubbed voraciously when she thought of all the indignities that had been forced upon her in one day. What she had suffered! Indeed, were the church nearby, she would be confessing to the Reverend for hours!

Grateful for the bath, she lay on the bed once she was satisfied she would not soil it, and Archie perched on the end rail of the bed. Out of the window, even she could make out that it was a beautiful estate, surrounded by a meadow and woodlands beyond it. Hattie had used to dream of the day she would be mistress of her own household, but in her heart had known she had most likely missed the chance when her father died and her mother's pastime of invalidity became reality.

A tear trickled down her cheek and she wiped it away with the back of her hand. Six-and-twenty was far too practical an age to be pining over silly romantic notions. However, there had to be some way to avoid living under this roof forever. Perhaps Richard would be willing to release her inheritance to her once she was out of mourning and he had accustomed himself to the notion of her as a spinster.

There was a knock on the door and Hattie realized her state of undress.

"Who is there?" she asked timidly.

"Why are you not dressed?" Louisa burst into the room in a frenzy of coquelicot silk trimmed with lace. Not enough to mind her assets, Hattie thought as she tried to focus her eyes somewhere other than her sister's expanse of skin. It only made her head ache more. Archie stood at attention, his feathers spread, and chattered in agitation, the sound low as though he were muttering. Louisa glared at him.

"I lost my trunks today. I only have the dress I travelled in and it is filthy. I set it aside for washing," Hattie explained.

"If you were not so high and mighty you would still have your trunks! You must dress for dinner," she said urgently, though making a clear effort to control her volume with the house full of guests. "Weston will expect you to be there, now, and I need you to even out the numbers," she hissed.

"I want no part of your fancy dinner or house party. Besides, I cannot go in my shift." Hattie crossed her arms defiantly.

"You ungrateful, unnatural girl!"

Archie growled, responding to her tone of voice, and Louisa jumped back.

"Control the damn bird or I will have him put in the dovecote!"

Hattie gasped at such vulgar language, and in particular from a lady. How dare she threaten poor Archie! She would find another situation in which to live as soon as she could speak with Richard.

"I will send my maid in with a gown. Do not make me also send Richard to speak some sense into you! He has enough to worry about with attending to his guests, as it is. We will be in the drawing room."

Hattie could tell it took a further effort for Louisa not to slam the door. She paced across the pink carpet, fretting as she awaited the maid and grumbling to herself, "I will go to dinner for my brother's sake, not Jezebel's—but I will not like it one bit, Archie."

The maid knocked before entering and stepped cautiously into the room while eyeing the bird with considerable suspicion. She held a gown of deep lavender and Hattie narrowed her eyes. Louisa knew she was still in mourning!

"This color will suit you, if I may say so, miss. My name is Sally."

"I cannot wear it. My mother has not been in the grave but six months."

"My mistress said you would object, but she says this is a small house party and it is all she has that will fit you. Lavender is still respectful to your mother, miss."

"If I do not wear it, she will send Richard up here and I do not wish to disturb my brother." Hattie held out her arms in resignation. No one would look at the old spinster, anyway.

The maid slipped the gown over Hattie's head and began to tie the laces up the back. Hattie scarcely wore anything fitted enough to require a maid's assistance. She looked down and saw her chest bulging over the top like a pair of pillows.

"I-I am indecent!" she cried.

Sally walked in front of her and looked. "Oh, no, miss. Your neckline is much higher than those of the other ladies. The color does suit you quite well. Sit down and I will dress your hair."

Hattie was not reassured at all as the maid led her to the dressing table before she could muster any more objections. She would try and find a shawl to cover herself before she went to the drawing room. The maid was brushing and twisting, and Hattie could not tell what was happening to her mousy locks, as her mother was wont to call them. Usually she kept them under a cap or bonnet.

"There you go, miss. Now we had best get you downstairs so my mistress won't be fretting," the maid said, placing slippers on Hattie's feet and ushering her out of the door. What she would not give to have her spectacles fixed! She could scarcely see five feet in front of her and was tempted to touch her coiffure to see what kind of exhibition she made from behind. It certainly felt as though she was exposed from her uncovered head to her indecent gown.

Sally escorted her down to the drawing room and Hattie could have sworn she was given a slight push through the door before it closed behind her. Feeling dizzy as she tried to focus on the room full of strangers, she began to sidle towards the far corner.

"Miss Longbottom." Lord Bergen's teasing voice spoke suddenly beside her and then he was taking her arm.

"My lord?" Hattie tried not to sound cold.

"You look...enchanting. Where is my dear friend, Archie?" He pretended to look about the room for him.

Louisa tittered as she glided up to join them. "Archie?"

"The popinjay. We are old acquaintances," he explained smoothly, sipping his drink.

"Are you indeed? How delightful," she cooed.

"Perhaps he can visit us after supper. Bentley, I was unaware you had a sister," Bergen remarked as he turned to Richard.

"Hattie has a different father. Our mother remarried when I was already away at school."

"And where did you acquire the delightful Archie, if I may be so bold?" Bergen asked, still that hint of mockery in his voice.

"He was a gift from my late father. He sometimes traveled to exotic lands," Hattie replied.

A stunning lady, dressed in a form-fitting dark green silk gown, moved closer to where they were. Hattie felt awkward and frumpy next to her.

"I beg your pardon... what is this? I heard exotic," she said with a low, husky voice.

"Lady Pennywaite, may I present my sister, Harriet Longbottom?" Bentley chimed in.

"How do you do?" Hattie said politely, suddenly feeling self-conscious next to this beautiful woman.

"I want to see this exotic creature!" Lady Pennywaite demanded.

"I am sure my sister will be happy to bring him down after dinner," Richard suggested as Hattie could see Louisa's jaw clench.

"The bird has to eat, too, does he not? Byron allows his bird to run tame and there are several at Chatsworth. One bird cannot do any harm," the woman said dismissively, clearly used to having her way.

"Hattie, would you mind bringing Archie to join us?" her brother asked.

"Shall we also set a place for him?" Louisa snapped, but Hattie took no notice and went to fetch the bird.

Praying that Archie would behave, Hattie reminded him to use good manners the entire way back to the drawing room. He made a purring sound in her ear as though he were listening, but the moment they walked through the drawing room doors, he screeched:

"Bugger! Whoremongers! Jezebel!"

"This gives the term popinjay a whole new meaning," Bergen drawled.

CHAPTER 4

*E*dward spotted Hampton returning from the balcony alone. *Finally, a chance to speak with him,* he thought. Just as he was approaching the man, dinner was announced and Hampton went straight to Lady Pennywaite, probably determined not to give Lord Purdy an opportunity to escort the young woman in to dinner. *Damn! I shall have to wait and he is avoiding me.* Knowing it would be a while before wine was served, Edward exchanged his empty glass for a full one. This was not going at all as he had hoped. He watched while several peers began escorting various ladies of obvious rank towards the dining room and noticed Miss Longbottom arrive, carrying Archie on her shoulder. *This should be interesting.* He permitted himself a wry smile.

He then noticed Lady Bentley immediately approaching her sister and the bird, so he stepped back out of sight but stayed within earshot, concerned for Miss Longbottom. He didn't care for the snippy antics of Lady Louisa Bentley.

"That is much better. I can see my old dress is a definite improvement, and provides the illusion of attributes. Perhaps I can find more gowns you can use. Yes, very good. I expect you to ensure that bird—" She narrowed her eyes, looking at Archie sitting on Hattie's shoulder.

"—behaves in a proper manner throughout the evening." On those words, she tossed her head back in a spiteful manner and walked in the direction of a group of ladies, across the room.

He recalled the gaudy bright red oriental wallpaper and dark furnishings from his earlier visit. *I still hate it.*

Edward was angry. He could not account for his defense of this woman, but her sister-in-law was a mean, spiteful biddy, and for some reason it infuriated him. He stepped in front of Louisa as she neared him, forestalling her. Smiling broadly, he extolled the virtues of her grand event.

"Lady Bentley, you have certainly outdone yourself with this party. I have noticed that your well-appointed affair has garnered not only most of the eligible men of the *ton*, but also many from the upper echelons of the peerage."

"Thank you, my lord. We are thrilled to have you join us," she cooed.

"My compliments," he responded with an ironic bow, knowing she would not recognize it as such. "Since my own rank is not your highest at the party, I have decided to escort Miss Longbottom in to dinner, Lady Eldon having withdrawn her attendance due to an inconvenient bout of influenza." A look of anger crossed her face, although it was quickly changed to one of serenity. He carefully kept his expression one of sincere appreciation.

"Of course, my lord. I was only now preparing to ask for your indulgence in escorting my dearest sister," she simpered, a smile firmly in place.

"I will be delighted to escort her." Without further exchange, he left to find Miss Longbottom and her feathered companion.

On finding that young lady, he approached her with his arm extended. "I would be honored if you would allow me to take you in to dinner, Miss Longbottom." He wanted to tell her she looked lovely; for she did. Her hair was softly curled, and the lavender dress complimented her color and her figure. The dress was much more fashionable, even if it appeared a little large.

"Thank you, my lord," she replied tentatively.

"I had quite forgotten that Archie would be joining us." He smiled at the bird. "Good evening Archie, I am so glad you could join us for dinner."

"Evening! Join dinner!" the bird cried out. Then he began nodding his head.

"Miss Longbottom, is Archie quite well? He appears to be behaving somewhat oddly this evening. He seems to be nodding in my direction. Could it signify anything?"

She looked up at him and smiled. He was taken back by the simple beauty he had not previously noticed. It was without any pretense and it caught him off guard.

"My lord, he does that when he likes someone. He is trying to let me know he approves of you."

"Well, that is something, indeed. He does seem... less... fractious." Edward could not imagine what had made the bird suddenly like him, and found it strange a bird could or would seek approval. It was intriguing—but then, he found practically everything about Archie amusing.

"Good evening to you both. Well, old friend, I see you have cornered our lovely Miss Longbottom." Bergen appeared from somewhere behind them.

"I have. Lady Bentley made a point of discussing the evenness of her guest list." Edward chuckled. "Indeed, I think the young lady on the settee requires an escort." Nodding towards the petite brunette, he urged Bergen to attend upon her. He enjoyed his friend, but tonight he was not in the mood for Bergen's gibes towards Miss Longbottom. He could not understand the protectiveness he felt, and had no desire to discuss it. What he was in the mood for was a fresh drink. He glanced around and spotting a footman with wine, signaled to him.

"I believe that the furnishings have not changed since I was here years ago." Edward could not regard the red Oriental paper, and the matching Aubusson carpet under the table, without wincing. He hoped that Bentley's circumstances had improved, recalling a visit he had made here with his parents a little above five years before. His mother had been very ungracious about the badly watered-down beverages, including the dinner wine. So far, if the brandy from this afternoon was any indication, Bentley's stock had improved substantially. He sipped his claret and relaxed. He recalled the exchange between Bentley and his wife this afternoon, when Miss Longbottom arrived. Their relationship was not unlike the cold and pretentious example set by his own parents.

Archie flapped his wings and brought him out of his reverie. "Ahem. I believe that Archie's seat is over there." Edward pointed to a high flower stand, set up behind a chair for the popinjay. *A space had actually been cleared at the table for the bird.* He fought the urge to laugh. "Let me see...ah yes, your seat is next to Archie, and mine is...on the other side of Archie." He spotted Hampton, seated across from them. Lady Pennywaite was sitting between Hampton and Purdy. *Someone has a strange sense of humor.* He fought an urge to glare at the man. Bergen had taken the chair on Miss Longbottom's right. The episode with her sister-in-law earlier had been very unsettling for the young woman, and he hoped to shield her from further upset—and that protective feeling, in itself, he found most disconcerting. Glancing down the table, he observed Lady Bentley, sitting at the south end of the table. The shrew's ire over Archie's presence was unmistakable; no one could miss her clenched jaw. Edward was glad that the woman was away from her sister-by-marriage. *This could be a long...interesting...evening,* he mused, avoiding catching Bergen's eye. He knew only too well where that would lead.

Dinner progressed slowly through the first few courses, but without incident. It seemed boring without the bird's shockingly delightful antics. Turning to address a comment to Miss Longbottom, he glimpsed Archie on his perch and noticed that the popinjay was staring back at him. The hairs on the back of his neck prickled.

Archie must have felt generous, because he began taking his food and fluttering down to place it on Edward's plate. The bird's feed mixture was now in his potato concoction, and Archie was fawning in an obscene manner along his arm, clawing it gently.

"My Lord! Mine!" he called as he stroked Edward's arm with his beak. Everyone in the room laughed and guffawed.

"Remove that bird at once!" Lady Bentley stood up and banged on her glass.

"Jezebel! Termagant!" Archie shrieked his message as he flapped his wings, green feathers flying. "Devil woman!" His cries were barely heard above the howls of laughter.

"Archie, please stop." Miss Longbottom worked feverishly snapping her fingers, trying to urge her bird back onto her shoulder.

"My lord, I apologize. I have no idea what has Archie so stirred up. He is being so naughty. I assure you, he is not usually so."

"Miss Longbottom, I fear your bird has provided more laughter and entertainment than this house has seen for years. Take a look at the head of the table." He gestured towards the far end of the table, where her brother was almost in tears.

"Indeed! It appears Lord Bentley is enjoying the entertainment." Bergen grinned and nodded in the same direction. "How delightful. I think our friend Archie has turned our dull house party into an absolute riot!"

Obviously enjoying the attention, Archie moved back to his perch, and then on to Bergen's shoulder. The bird immediately nuzzled his head into Bergen's neck and began giving what appeared to be affectionate pecks on his ear.

"Very good. Good!" Archie cooed, bobbing his head gently against Bergen's cheek.

For a moment, Edward was slack-jawed, as a sudden irrational jealousy towards Bergen thrummed through his body. Realizing his mouth hung open, he closed it, and quickly contrived a look of amusement, wondering what had come over him.

Miss Longbottom struggled to keep her bird on her shoulder when she rose and attempted to make her apologies for having to leave with a headache.

"You...you! And that mangy, ill-conceived, ill-mannered bird!" Lady Bentley was suddenly in front of Miss Longbottom, gesticulating wildly.

"Get out of my sight." the woman screeched. Her voice was more piercing than the parrot's. "You have ruined my party."

Hattie reached up, and holding Archie in place, turned to leave.

"Ruined! Mangy! Jezebel!" By now extremely nervous—even to Edward's unknowledgeable eye—Archie flapped and shrieked as the room's noise level increased further. The bird spit at Louisa, barely missing her.

"Allow me. What kind of escort would I be if I permitted my dinner partner to leave by herself under these circumstances?" Edward offered his arm and together, they left the room.

He was anxious to get to his own bedchamber, but wanted to visit the card room in search of Hampton. During the disturbance, the man had slipped from the dining room, in company with Lady Pennywaite.

Archie surprised him by jumping to his shoulder and rubbing his head against Edward's face, calling him, "Whoremonger" in an affectionate fashion. Even Miss Longbottom had to laugh.

Sally was already halfway downstairs to help Hattie. "Come, miss, let us get upstairs before the Mistress sees us."

Miss Longbottom lifted Archie from his shoulder and, as he stood watching, walked up two stairs before turning.

"Thank you for your kindness, my lord."

He inclined his head and watched her walk on, pursing his lips in disbelief at the uproar this woman and her bird had caused in one day.

Crossing the hall, he slipped into the card room, where games of whist and piquet were beginning. The smell of spent tobacco hung in the air. Brass wall sconces lined the dark green and cream wallpapered walls, and iron and glass chandeliers hung over square rosewood card tables. The players relaxed in comfortable ram's head side chairs, while several spectators stood watching over their shoulders.

Three or four drinks later—he was not counting—he finally had a chance to gain Hampton's attention.

"Lord Hampton, a moment, please."

His brother's friend faced him. "Yes, Weston. You wish to speak with me?"

"I will not mince words. I want to hear from you what happened on the night my brother was killed. Please do not insult my intelli-

EARL OF WESTON

gence by telling me he lost a duel. We both know that the shot went wide. He was killed by a bullet through his side." The man began to fidget.

"You must be mistaken, my lord. Your brother fell when the shots were fired." He looked over his shoulder, and then, back. "What do you believe happened?"

Edward could feel his anger and frustration brewing. He started to answer when the door opened and in walked Lord Bentley, with a guest he had not seen arrive.

"Ladies, gentlemen...may I introduce my wife's brother, Mr. Philip Martin?"

A corpulent, balding man stood at Lord Bentley's side. His clothing looked shabby, and his neck cloth hung in disarray. Martin had a strange tightness about his mouth.

The room went silent. Edward noticed Hampton leave hurriedly, wearing a look of alarm. He was not sure what to make of it. He also noticed that Lord Bentley quickly made an introduction, to the couple closest to his brother-by-marriage, engaging them in conversation, and then moved slowly towards the group playing whist in the far corner of the room. *Interesting. Bentley doesn't favor his brother-in-law.*

"Bergen," Edward said, strolling over to greet him. "There you are my friend. How is it that your game has already ended? I am afraid I have failed on all fronts with Hampton. What do you say we join a game and try our luck?"

"Happy to, Weston. I was just watching the table in the back there." He pointed to the table that was having a loud discussion. "I predict that game will end quickly, just as mine did."

"Heavens! What did you do to have the whole table abandon you?" Edward snickered, and then lightly slapped his friend's back in a sign of familiarity.

"I am not sure, exactly. I thought perhaps it was to start with games for larger groups."

Four games later, Edward was ready to call it a night. The brandy had been excellent, but he had not only lost count of his money, he had also not tallied the drink he had consumed. The dull ache of his head urged him to go to bed. Bergen was still enjoying himself, obviously winning his hands.

Edward was tired. It had been a full day. He pushed back from the table and found his thoughts going back to the curious Miss Longbottom and her parrot. He had to admit, she was not as bad as he had first considered. He glanced around the room, wondering if any of the earls present might consider her for a match—certainly not the type for himself, but someone else might find her so.

Slowly, he made his way upstairs. In a fleeting thought, he wondered what room had been assigned to Miss Longbottom. Opening his dark room, he noticed the fire had burned down. The room had just the right amount of coolness to it, so he decided to forgo building up the fire. He just wanted sleep. Sitting on the nearest chair, he pulled off his boots and then the rest of his clothes. They lay scattered on the floor where they landed. Without bothering to search his baggage for a night-shift, he pulled back the covers and slipped between the noticeably warm sheets. The smell of rose and a comfortable bed took his thoughts back to a ride with a firm young woman pushed up against him on his mount. *Warm sheets are divine*, he thought, turning towards the warmer side of the bed. It was his last thought before he dropped off to sleep.

Hattie fell into bed feeling humiliated and exhausted. Sally had lent her a flannel night-dress and a lovely pair of wool socks she had knitted herself. Hattie was certain she would never have been able to sleep in just her shift.

Hopefully, when she woke, she would be back in her warm bed in Little Whitley and dreaming of her day's activities as one of the Lord's helpers in the parish. Never before today could she have imagined how out of place she would feel in her brother's household.

Every young girl dreams of what it must be like to sit at a table with London's elite, but it had been nothing like her imaginings. It was certainly unlike any of the social gatherings at home. For one, the gowns the ladies wore left nothing to the imagination and those same gentlewomen flirted and fawned shamelessly over the gentlemen. Their behavior was much as her mother had once described the flagrancy of ladies of the night! If that were not enough to offend every sensibility, there was far too much imbibing of liquor taking place.

Hattie had walked into a den of Hades. It was all due to Jezebel, she had no doubt. Richard was a very fine man. Even if she had not been raised with him, he had always been very good and kind to her. It was enough to put her off for her food. She yawned as sleepiness overcame her, her last thought a resolution to speak to Richard about it first thing in the morning.

Hattie could scarcely ever recall a dream after she awoke. Occasionally she could remember one from her youth, when she had hopes of a handsome squire galloping down the drive to carry her away to his country estate. Naturally, a brood of children followed and they lived happily ever after. Perhaps, on occasion, there had been a chaste kiss on the lips...

Tonight, however, she was having a dream unlike any other she had experienced before. She was in the marriage bed—and it involved sensations no decent woman had any right to feel!

Her tall, and very muscular, husband was kissing her neck and tracing his tongue slowly around her ear. She could not see his face, but he smelled of cloves, smoke, and spirits. She had smelled that scent somewhere before. It was oddly disorientating yet also comforting. Strange, warm sensations were shooting through her body, settling deep within; a burning, tingling feeling... *there*. Then, through the flannel of her night-dress, his hands were caressing her everywhere. Part of her knew she should be shocked, yet somehow she could not find the strength, even when she felt an exquisite pain in her chest. She writhed away from him in an attempt to make the feeling go away, but he drew her back. One of his hands slid down her body and slowly, sensuously, lifted her gown to her neck. Moist kisses replaced the rub of his hand and she shuddered, barely noticing as his fingers travelled over her skin. Teasing caresses stroked her... and a

ANNA ST. CLAIRE & WITH LAUREN HARRISON

moan escaped her lips. She twisted against the knowing, wicked touch. Why could she not wake up from this dream? Suddenly, her husband's warm, heavy body covered hers, and then, through her subconscious, she realized that this was not a dream. *I have no husband!* her mind cried out.

She attempted to sit up and panicked as she found her night-rail was around her neck, entangling her. Desperately, she struggled to be free.

Wide-eyed with horror, she felt something warm and firm slide against her thigh.

"Snake!" she cried. "Help!" Jumping out of the bed, she grabbed her pillow and began beating the mattress as her night-rail found its way back downward.

Archie let out a loud, shrill, sound of distress. "Help! Help!"

"Hell and damnation!" The man bellowed the words as he jumped away from her and began to fumble in the dark.

"Whoremonger!" Archie greeted the familiar intruder from under his blanketed cage.

The door to her room burst open and there stood Richard, holding a taper and looking furious. Before long, most of the house appeared to be standing outside her door.

Hattie quickly checked her night-dress was fully down, leaped back into the bed and pulled the covers over her head. She had never been more ashamed or mortified. How could her life have plummeted into the depths of complete depravity in the course of four-and-twenty hours?

She heard Louisa exclaim, in a dramatic fashion, "To think we allowed the harlot under our roof!"

Hattie seethed with anger.

"Louisa, hush. Weston?" Her brother spoke with eerie calm.

"I beg your pardon, Bentley. There has been a dreadful mistake. I will, however, be leaving for London at first light."

"See that you do."

Hattie tried to peek at the scene she could envision only too well. She could see very little more than her brother's back as he commanded everyone back to bed, and Jezebel's beady eyes glaring at her.

The door closed with a resounding snap and Hattie suddenly wished everyone would come back. She could not face this man, knowing what they had done.

"Well, madam, can you not look at your future groom?"

She shook her head underneath the covers.

She heard him curse under his breath before sitting on the bed. The mattress dipped beneath his weight and she had difficulty in maintaining her position. She sucked in her breath. Did he intend...?

"Miss Longbottom. Oh, the devil! What is your name?" he muttered.

"H-Ha—Hattie," she squeaked.

"Hattie. Please allow me to speak to your face."

She was completely unprepared for such a situation and how to handle it. Her education as a young lady had been sorely lacking in this particular area. However, she had been brought up to look people in the eye when they spoke to her. She slowly lowered the blanket from her face but held it tightly under her chin. Her cap was askew and she could see strands of hair hanging in wild disarray. What a sight she must be!

"Yes, my lord?" she asked testily. This mess was all his doing, the blackguard.

"Edward. My name is Edward," he said softly. "May I humbly beg your pardon? I know it is too little too late, but I drank too much and entered your room by mistake."

She could feel her mouth hanging open. How could he sit on her bed unclothed and expect a tête-à-tête?

"I will obtain a special license and we may be married in three days' time."

"I do not want to marry you," she growled.

"Be that as it may, there are few options. Would you prefer living with Jezebel? I assure you, madam, that I would not cast you away as a maid."

"No, I am aware of that, sir," she acknowledged quietly. "You have shown me generosity. It is only—I do not wish to live a fashionable life. We do not suit in that regard."

"We suit in another," he rasped. He was much too close for her comfort. She could clearly see how handsome he was, and it was hard not to stare at his muscular chest and arms, and the expanse of hair down to his... Hattie's cheeks flushed with remembrance of the feel of that coarse hair chafing her own bare flesh.

"You will have three days to accustom yourself to the idea of being my countess. If you find you cannot countenance me, you may live alone in the country—once you have conceived—and tolerate me from time to time. I give you fair warning, I will be a part of my children's lives. I assure you, I will not be an unreasonable husband. His gaze was unnerving as he watched her, presumably to make sure she understood.

He then rose and gathered his clothing before leaving for his own room, leaving her to squint after his well-proportioned form.

CHAPTER 5

*E*dward had planned to leave at first light. It was actually half past seven when he and Bergen departed. A brief meeting with Bentley on his plans had turned into half an hour, with Edward discussing his plans for settlements. Bentley was more than pleased. Edward had lain awake in his own bed the night before, cogitating about his situation and waiting for sleep to overtake him. He wanted to behave in an honorable manner, and the more he thought about marriage to Hattie Longbottom, the more resigned he became.

He considered it would take the better half of the day to reach London. He had several stops to make, including speaking with his mother. He was dreading that. On the one hand, his having to be married should please her, but he knew his mother. She was a parvenu and not only would she find fault with his intended, but she would harp on about how Hattie's breeding not being good enough for the Weston line. It was her way of controlling her children and inserting herself into their lives—blasting them with her requirements until they acquiesced. Robert had deplored her interference and continually lamented their parent's review of the women he had spent time with, to the point where he had avoided family parties whenever he had been able.

To his surprise, Bergen volunteered to accompany him to London, and he was glad to have his company. One day he would tell Bergen how much his friendship meant to him, but that would wait until after he had begged a favor. Edward glanced over at Bergen and smiled. Yes, he needed to get that out of the way, first.

"Tell me, Weston. You are off to the archbishop to obtain a special license, you have to face your mother, and you are having to see your solicitor—not to mention you are being leg-shackled in three days." Bergen shook his head. "Please...do tell me again about the snake? The announcement of its arrival roused half the wing." He laughed so loudly, his horse tossed his head and snorted in irritation.

They were several hours into their trip. The road was dusty, and cut through farmland, so they didn't have the cover of trees at this juncture. He sensed that Bergen was holding back, but he refused to bring up the subject of Miss Longbottom. They had spoken about every topic except her—or his situation. He was confident that Bergen would not remain silent too much longer. Edward glanced over and caught the smirk on Bergen's face, and knew this trip was going to get the better of him. He tried to shake off his irritation, but could not. "You need me to say it again? Very well, I will. I over-imbibed. I put myself in bed, as I always do. Damn it! If you are going to harass me..." He stopped. He did not want to alienate his friend. After all, he had only himself to blame. On top of that, if it had happened to Bergen, he would also be relentless in jocular harassment. "Perhaps I should have abstained from the last glass of brandy. It was just too good to waste; and yes, it will be difficult dealing with my mother. On top of all that..."

Bergen cut him off. "Weston, it is none of my business. I must, however, say this. You have a problem. In a world of dipping too deep, you drink to excess. You are my best friend and are like a brother to me, which is why I must put you straight, no matter the cost. Do not glare at me. Someone has to say it. I also enjoy a good drink and a night on the spree, but you do not seem to know when to stop. It has thrust you into more than one scrape—and now this... Honestly, you are getting leg-shackled and it is because you were foxed." He paused for breath. "In this case, even though it looks disastrous, Miss Long-bottom could be the very thing for you. I think there is a lot more to her than meets the eye."

At last allowed to speak, Edward responded with considerable testiness.

"You insult me, Bergen. I will, however, concede you make a valid point. I do think Hattie could be good for me. She will provide me with a much-needed heir, which will fulfill my mother's need and make her cease her constant haranguing."

Bergen shook his head.

"I have a favor to ask." Edward felt annoyed. He had to admit, at least to himself, that he had swigged far too much. He had been as drunk as a wheelbarrow and made a quick, mental note not to do so again. Meanwhile, he still needed to make his request. "We should be in London by supper-time if we do not stop longer than it takes to rest the horses. An hour, maybe two."

Bergen merely nodded.

"My friend," Edward remarked with a smile, "you are showing more signs of fatigue than I, and I am the one caught in the wrong room."

"Yes, about that. I am still curious about that..." Bergen shot his friend a mischievous look. "Snake?"

Edward could not help but laugh. "Yes, well my...snake...had a pleasant reaction to the warmth coming from the other side of the bed." He forced a lascivious smirk. It was curious, yet the memory lacked such humor. "How was I to know she was in the room? It was dark." He thought for moment, recalling the moment of realization that he was sharing her bed, and shuddered.

"By Jove, the whole house collected in the hallway to see our misery; and Lady Louisa...decent words fail me. Now that you mention it, I did not see you. Where, my friend, *were* you?" He sneered to emphasize the veiled jibe. "Did you know she tried to kill the... snake? She used a pillow to...batter me."

Bergen nearly choked. Then he roared with laughter. "I was sleeping."

"Yes, I gathered that. Let me try to guess where." He looked up sharply into his friend's cheery face. "No! Tell me you did not, Bergen!" Edward was incredulous. "The lady practically caused a duel with Hampton and Purdy over dinner...and you just swooped in for the night? Do you believe she will stay silent?"

"Yes. That she will."

"Oh. I see. It was not the first time." He snorted. "Well, she is a widow, at least, so Society will look the other way. It is not so with Hattie."

"I think you will suit," Bergen offered.

"Maybe. It does not matter; however; I do find I hold a fascination for her—if not with that molting, obnoxious bird."

"You are still put out that he flirted with you at dinner." Bergen snorted rudely and spurred his horse.

Edward also urged his horse faster. He was not about to allow Bergen to have the final word on the subject. He would never hear the end of it—and he still needed to ask him that favor. Some yards further on, he pulled up alongside his friend.

"You misinterpreted Archie's behavior, Bergen. Very well. Let's say it was a little embarrassing. And were you not also discomfited over his adoration?" Edward snorted. "That brings me to a favor I need to ask of you. I have noticed the camaraderie that you and Archie share."

"Absolutely not! Weston, I do not need a bird. And if I did, I would not want *that* bird—even though he does provide abundant entertainment." He gestured wildly, mocking the parrot's actions.

Edward gave a wolfish grin and watched his friend squirm for a moment or two.

"Not permanently, Bergen." He laughed. "Just for the first week or so. I am not able to...carry through...if you get my meaning."

Bergen raised his eyes heavenwards and spurred his horse faster without answering.

"So, is that a yes?" He urged his own mount on and the two men picked up speed for London.

~

The meeting with the archbishop could not have gone better. He had the special license safety tucked into his pocket. There were a few more matters he wanted to attend to before his return journey. Edward rode into Ludgate Hill and stopped at Rundell & Bridge. He had decided to forego the usual signet ring that most exchanged and find something a little more suitable—perhaps something that showed off her eyes, a feature he found he really liked.

The bell jingled, announcing his visit. A bespectacled, aged gentleman with greying hair looked up from a microscope and welcomed him. They had met many times before.

"Lord Weston. How nice to see you, my lord! What can I do for you today?"

"Mr. Benton, thank you. I have an errand which brings me here today."

"I can tell from your smile that this must be a special lady."

Smile? Am I smiling? He had not realized that he had been smiling. He had to admit that the longer he had had to think about it, the more he was looking forward to this marriage.

"Yes, I am to be married, and I have need of a ring," he informed the goldsmith. Robert had bequeathed to him his signet ring, but Edward wanted to keep that. It was not suitable for a lady, anyway. Edward scanned the cases, his gaze stopping on a display of sapphire rings. "Ah! Right here. I think sapphires would become her."

"It is an excellent choice for a ring, my lord. Sapphires symbolize wisdom, virtue, sincerity, faithfulness, and good fortune. It is a beautiful stone. What do you think of this one?" Pulling out a slender, rose gold band with diamond and sapphire baguettes, he held it up to Edward. "It is a vibrant blue. What is your opinion, sir?"

"It is simple and beautiful, and as you say, there is a vibrancy to it. I shall take it. Do you have a necklace and earrings to match with it?" The sapphires reminded him of Hattie's eyes. Of a certainty, sapphires would suit her. She was the most forthright person he had met in a long time, so a stone symbolizing sincerity went well with her character. How strange, he mused, thinking of her gave him this odd feeling, almost a longing. "That is silly. I barely know her," he chastised himself, aloud.

"I beg your pardon, my lord?" The old man looked up from the case of jewelry.

"Forgive me. I have ridden all day and was just reflecting on what I wanted to achieve. I did not realize I spoke the thought. I would like the matching earrings and necklace, too."

"Yes, my lord. Shall I put these purchases on your account and wrap them for you?" The jeweler hastened to begin wrapping the jewelry.

"Yes, thank you. No, wait, please." He spotted eyeglasses in a corner case. "Mr. Benton, would you assist me with a pair of these spectacles?"

"As you wish, my lord." He selected a pair of oval lady's spectacles with rose gold rims and held them up for Edward's scrutiny. "Do these meet with your approval, my lord?"

Edward took the glasses and held them up. Things looked fuzzy to him. "I cannot be sure. Are things always fuzzy?"

"I am told that for those who cannot see far away, these help, my lord."

He pictured Hattie with her squint, and suddenly realized how difficult it was for her. If these glasses would help her, it could make life easier. She probably could not see anything past the nose on her face. *How strenuous that must be,* he thought. *And I doubt she ever complains.* "Yes, I think those will do." He imagined Hattie's face when he gave her the glasses and grinned. "These will do nicely. Thank you, Mr. Benton."

Hurrying with his purchases, he realized he was to meet Bergen at the club shortly. Thank goodness Bergen had agreed to watch Archie for a few days. He started with a couple of weeks, and finally got what he needed—four nights without the popinjay. Hattie would probably object. But he couldn't spend the first nights of his marriage watched by a shrieking bird.

Hattie was not about to leave her room. Humiliation did not begin to describe her feelings and she did not want everyone staring at her. She could not keep them from gossiping, however. The only improper thing she had done was to be in the wrong room at the wrong time! Well, perhaps she had participated a little in her dream but she had not done it consciously!

Lord Weston—Edward—had left for London early. She had not slept and had heard him ride away. From the clatter of hooves, it had sounded as though he must have taken Lord Bergen with him, so her only remaining ally would be Richard. That was not enough to convince her to face the approbation.

There was a soft knock on her door. She ignored it; she had no intention of answering. Jezebel would march into the room whether she was welcome or not.

"Hattie?" her brother inquired as he looked around the door.

"Richard. Come in." If she had to talk to someone, she would rather it be him.

"May we speak about last night? Weston explained what happened and it is most unfortunate. How are you faring?" he asked kindly.

"Well enough." Her voice cracked and she swallowed as she sat stroking Archie's head.

"He is an honorable man, Hattie. I should have warned you to lock your door. House parties are often known for their night-time liaisons, and people often drink more than is wise."

Hattie looked up in shock at her brother, who shrugged.

"It is the way of the world, Hattie. I wish I had taken you from mother much sooner. She could have lived here and you could have had your proper entry into Society. Instead, you have been sheltered and are as naïve as a girl still in the school room."

"I most certainly am not! Reverend Hastings warned me about the pleasures of the flesh. I choose to live a pure and devout life."

"It was not my intention to imply you could not be either. Nevertheless, as Weston's wife, you will have certain obligations as a hostess. He has been very generous towards you. He must have stayed awake and written up the settlements for you. He said he would have his solicitor draw up the formal agreement while he is in Town."

Hattie did not know what to say.

"I only hope, dear sister, that you will give him a chance to make a proper marriage and not hide away in the country. His brother was killed less than a year ago in suspicious circumstances. He was never intended to be the Earl and is having a rather difficult time of it. I know you are capable of being a good wife to him."

"Must I host parties such as this, where people drink too much and share each other's beds?"

Richard sighed loudly. "I cannot say what your husband will choose to do, Hattie. Not everyone is so fortunate in their marriage as your mother and father were. Many of our class are forced to marry to support our estates."

"And so seek pleasures elsewhere?" she asked, knowing she must be wide-eyed with shock.

"I am afraid it is so. It would be best to disguise your astonishment."

"I want to be a good wife," she said meekly, while rubbing Archie from his head down his tail.

"I knew you would. Shall I take you into Oxford today, to find you a gown for your wedding? Louisa has agreed to lend Sally to you."

Hattie could only imagine Louisa "agreeing."

"Thank you, Richard. I confess, I would appreciate having some of my own clothing."

"I will be downstairs with the carriage when you are ready, then."

Richard left and Sally entered soon after to help her to dress. She was holding Hattie's freshly washed, crêpe day gown.

"I hope you do not mind accompanying me. I do need your assistance. My brother says I need to make an effort to be a good wife to Weston, but I have no notion of how to go on; about what might be fashionable."

"I have been to London many times with Lady Bentley. It is my duty to know the latest mode." She helped Hattie out of her night-rail and slipped her day dress over her head. "First, we will find something which fits you. No more cast-off dresses for you, miss. We could fit two of you in here." She tightened the laces, but it was still like a sack-cloth on her.

"It seemed wasteful to ruin my own clothes with black dye for mourning. Now they are lost to me." She sat at the dressing table and allowed Sally to dress her hair. Everything was still blurred without her glasses and she squinted hard to see what the maid was doing. Her hair had never looked pretty before—she had always worn a severe plait under a cap.

"One more thing, miss... you cannot squint like that. Forgive my saying so, but it is not the most flattering pose."

Hattie leaned forward to peer into the looking-glass and sat back with an exclamation when she saw how her nose wrinkled and her lip curled upward.

"Oh! How dreadful!"

The maid nodded. "Let us be going, then. We have much to do."

"Be a good boy, Archie," Hattie called as they left.

"Good boy! Good boy!" he said, bobbing his head up and down.

CHAPTER 6

*E*dward dreaded his next meeting. His mother was not his favorite companion. She would be difficult, at best. "Hilton, is my mother at home?" He stood at the opened threshold of his family's town residence, hesitating before entering the house.

"May I take your coat and hat, my lord?"

He allowed the servant to relieve him of the heavy outerwear. The aging butler hung up the coat and then nodded at Edward.

"She is in her parlor, my lord."

"Thank you." Edward took a fortifying breath and made his way to his mother's sitting room and knocked. "Mother?" He opened the door and walked in.

"Oh, Edward. You decided to visit. How nice." His mother looked up from her book. "I had heard you had gone to Eynsham, not that you ever tell me what you are about." She shot him an austere look and went back to reading.

"Mother, I have important news and a request." Edward fought his impatience and kept his outer composure, while his insides churned.

"You have a request? Do go on." She remained focused on the open pages in front of her.

Edward lost patience. She could read 'Othello' when he left. He walked over to his mother and pulled her volume closed.

"How dare you? What do you think you are doing, Edward? I did not bring you up to be rude." She snatched her tome back and opened it.

"You did not bring me up to be anything, Mother. You did not bring me up at all. However, let us not worry ourselves with such details. I am getting married. I came to tell you." He hated to be so brusque with his mother, but she vexed him.

The book fell away and his mother stood up, a stunned look on her face. "May I ask who the young woman is? I feel sure you have mismanaged the whole affair and I will not have the Weston line sullied by any fortune-hunter who has set her cap at you, Edward." She screwed her face into an expression of distaste.

"Mother, whom I marry has little to do with your opinion." He bit his tongue and stopped before he threatened to move her to the Dowager cottage on the country estate.

She moved to the window and stood, staring outside, her arms crossed. Outside, the gardener was pruning the shrubs. The sound of his clippers could be heard above the silence in the room. "Must we argue, Edward? Your actions mock me at every turn. I have tried to do what is right for the family. It was you who failed us. I lost a son because of you. You should have been home to help him, but no! You were gallivanting in Paris, doing goodness knows what—gambling? Whoring, perhaps? Your behaviour was disgraceful. That is how, in my eyes, you compare to your brother. It should have been you."

Her icy words pummeled him, one by one. That his mother would even speak of such activities surprised him. But that was always part of her attack—to throw her opponent off and swoop in for the kill. Edward was determined not to let her gain control of this discussion. He felt his temper rising, and struggled to control it. While he understood that part of this was her grief speaking, a large amount was through an inner ugliness she reserved for his benefit. He could not remember when she had been nice to him, or praised him for anything. She had saved all of that for Robert. He was not jealous of his brother. He missed him and he loved him. *Just once, I wish Mother could show me some level of warmth.* It would never happen.

"Mother... I, too, think about Robert all the time. But the fact of the matter is he is gone and I am here. He called the duel, and lost it. You have one son now, and I am he. I am sorry you are disappointed, but be that as it may, I am taking a wife and you will treat her with the respect due to a countess. And..." He paused, taking a deep breath. "And you will meet her at the wedding, which is in two days. I bid you to have your trunk packed. I will return for you tomorrow." He bowed and turned to leave.

"You have not mentioned who she is." Her words stopped him, her voice almost a whisper.

"Her name is Harriet Longbottom—Hattie, Lord Bentley's sister. We are to be married at her brother's country estate."

"This cannot be happening!" His mother's face twisted in anger. "Lord Bentley's *half*-sister? How could you do *that* to this family! She is hardly deserving to kiss your family ring. Edward, you must reconsider. There are several diamonds of the first water on the market..."

"Enough! Mother, I do not wish to argue with you. Nor is it my wish to disappoint you. However, who I choose to marry is not your concern."

"I see. You were foxed and compromised her. I cannot believe you could have been interested in any relation of Louisa Bentley... and do not bother to lie to me. I can tell by your expression that you did just that. Consider your name and position..."

"Mother, the decision as to whom I wed is mine." He spoke slowly and deliberately. *Well, maybe not completely in this case.* How did she know how to get under his skin? Of course, she was right about what had happened and that added to his irritation. He fought for control of his words. "Hattie and I are betrothed. Furthermore, Mother, if you cannot be respectful and treat her with the kindness she deserves, we will not visit. You will live here in your town house, or in the Dower House in Hampshire. Do I make myself clear?"

They stared at each, until she looked away. "Very well," she muttered, looking away. "I will be ready. And," she sighed, "I will be...cordial to your bride. *I* know my duty." She pasted a cold smile on her face and spoke in a subdued tone.

He did not miss her derisive smile or her false tone. He expected it. This was her typical response to any request he made. However, he chose not to take the bait. "Mother, it has been interesting, as always." He placed a kiss on her cheek, and noticed she did not react. "I think you will like her, if you will give her a chance." Even he did not believe what he had just said. "My carriage will be here at seven o'clock on the morrow to pick you up. Please be ready."

"I will." Her tone remained derisive.

"Good."

"Before you make your grand exit, Edward, I found something in your brother's effects that I thought you might be able to clear up for me." She leafed through to the back of her book and withdrew a folded piece of vellum. "Here!" She shoved the note in his hands. "Maybe you can make sense of it."

Edward started to read the note.

"It is from some man I did not recognize...he signed it Martin, I believe. He requested a meeting with Robert, regarding your gambling debts that he wanted covered. I believe the dates he mentioned are also in there. They were accumulated the week before Robert's death, at some club or such in London."

Edward stared at the note a moment longer. He had not been in the country that week. He wanted to show this to Bergen, to see what he thought of it. It had to be a connection to Robert's death—he could feel it. He just did not know what that connection could be. He tucked the note into his jacket pocket.

"Thank you, Mother. I will look into this." His voice softened. "These are not debts I created."

"I could not say." She was looking away from him again.

"Well, as I say, I plan to look into this, but I am not going to bother defending myself to you. It is a waste of my time." He paused. "I will see you tomorrow, Mother. Let us hope for pleasant weather."

Satisfied that things would go as well as they could with his mother, he left for his other town house. *His home.* He had arranged to meet Bergen at the Club, in a couple of hours, for dinner, and he wanted to change his raiment. Bergen had mentioned celebrating Edward's upcoming nuptials. *I could use a good brandy or two.* It would be good to have a quiet night at the club. As he mounted his horse, he thought more about that note. He wondered what Robert would say about all of this.

~

Hattie had never owned anything so lavish or extravagant in her life, she decided, as she saw her reflection in the glass. A well-proportioned woman, in a high-waisted lavender silk gown with a shimmering overdress and dainty capped sleeves, looked back at her. In fact, this gown cost more than the sum of her lifetime's worth of dresses! She felt like a beautiful princess, but a guilty one. They had never been poor; in fact, Hattie knew she had a dowry which would become her own competence if she did not marry by the age of thirty.

"Don't you look a picture, miss!" Sally said from somewhere behind her.

Tears sprang into Hattie's eyes as she realized what a change was about to take place. She was terrified. She was no more suited to be a countess, regardless of her genteel upbringing, than Lord Weston was suited to be in the church. They were from two entirely different worlds and this was nothing short of a disaster! Her cheeks heated when she recalled the feeling of his mouth and hands on her—*when he had not realized whom he was touching*, she thought bitterly. Admittedly, she had responded to his touch, but would it be enough to prevent their marriage being a misery? To keep it from being nothing more than an empty show put on for Society?

"What is the matter, miss?" Sally asked. "You are supposed to be delighted. Is this not what every lady dreams about? Lord Weston is the most handsome man I have ever seen. And he treats his dependents well, from what I've heard tell."

"Oh, Sally. It was a horrible mistake. He does not wish to marry me!"

"Then I suppose he should have considered that before he climbed into your bed!"

Hattie stood with her jaw hanging open at the maid's impertinence. Never would one of her mother's servants have had the audacity to say such a thing—even if what she said was correct.

The maid was still talking. "It is the way of the world and if he was not to marry you, you would be ruined. I have seen that happen as well and you should be thankful Lord Weston is an honorable gentleman."

"Why is he being lauded as honorable for coming into my bed and compromising me?" Hattie snapped.

"As my mistress said, if such a rumpus had not been raised, then it could have been kept quiet."

"So, now the whole sordid affair becomes my fault?" Hattie asked, incredulous.

"Now then, don't fly up into the boughs right before your wedding. As my ma always said, 'What's done is done and now you make the best of it.'"

"A charming start to any union," Hattie muttered in defiance, but she was most afraid of what came after the ceremony. Granted, she had not known anything the other night and things had progressed regardless, but instinct told her there was more than what had happened.

"Sally?"

"Yes, miss? I am almost finished now." She put a few more pins in Hattie's hair.

"Have you ever... do you know... oh, how do I ask this?" Hattie threw up her hands.

Sally stepped in front of her and smiled. "You mean the wedding night? But I thought..."

"How could you think that?" she asked, dropping her hands on her hips.

"I am sure I do not know, miss." Sally chuckled.

Hattie's shoulders slumped. "Well, we were, but when I felt his... his... snake..."

"Oh lawks! So you truly did call it a snake!" Sally burst out laughing and kept laughing until she was holding her sides and crying.

"Sally!" Hattie snapped, in an attempt to bring the maid out of her merriment.

"I am sorry," she sighed, still smiling. "That is the funniest story I have heard in my life."

"I am happy to know you enjoyed my distress, but do be serious for a moment. I need to know what happens. The Bible mentions joining, but how does it happen?"

"Well, now, miss. How do you think it happens?"

Hattie thought for a moment and shock registered on the face staring back at her from the looking-glass when she realized the snake's purpose.

"Oh no," she whispered.

"Yes. But don't you worry, it will fit."

"I do not want it to fit!" she protested.

"You will, mark my words." Sally winked. "And almost any other female in the country would, too. You had best appreciate what you've been given."

The maid's words did not make her feel at all better. She could not stop thinking about what was going to happen to her and regretted asking. Lord Weston had made it clear he wanted heirs, so there was no hope for a marriage in name only. She was sick to her stomach at the thought she would have to face him during the ceremony, knowing what was to come. All of those people would be watching her, knowing what they had done and knowing she was not sophisticated enough for him.

"Stop worrying yourself to flinders. His lordship knows what he is doing. Just let him do what he wants and all will be well."

Hattie expelled a deep breath and reminded herself she wanted to be a good wife. Being submissive to someone else was going to be difficult after six and twenty years without such constraints.

"Now you look the perfect bride—so long as you don't squint."

"So long as I do not trip or run into the altar," Hattie added.

There was a knock on the door and Sally let Richard inside.

"Sister, you are beautiful!" he exclaimed. She smiled despite her nerves.

"Thank you, Richard. I have never owned anything so dear," she confessed.

"That circumstance was a dreadful oversight on my part. This *toilette* was worth every penny. I trust the other gowns were delivered with this one?"

"Yes, you were very generous, brother."

"I very much enjoyed spending the day with you, Hattie. I hope, once you are settled, we may join our families together on better terms. Louisa will come about. If nothing else, you will outrank her," he teased. "Are you ready to be married?"

"May I answer honestly?" Hattie responded, looking up at her brother.

"Perhaps I should put it another way. Everything will work out for the best. You will see, dear Hattie. I do not believe in accidents. All things happen for a reason, and I truly think you and Weston were intended for each other."

"I can scarce credit that my brother sounds so wise."

"Your brother has been married to Louisa for ten years."

"And this has made you wiser?" she asked skeptically.

"Indeed. You can choose to make the best of any situation."

"I suppose so." She smiled sheepishly up at him.

"One last piece of advice," he said as they walked through the house. "Find Archie his own room to sleep in."

Richard had insisted upon them having the ceremony at the church. Despite the inauspicious beginning, he wanted to imagine a love match. Hattie was entirely too practical for that. She was no beauty like Lady Pennywaite, though Sally had managed to work a miracle with her appearance in three short days. Never would she become accustomed to having her bosom on display; she could even see them without looking, although they were less conspicuous than those belonging to most ladies.

Richard handed her down from the carriage and escorted her up the steps to the church. Before the doors were opened to the nave, a place where Hattie was normally most comfortable, she felt guilty about crossing the threshold. This wedding was a farce—except it was still happening.

The bells chimed the hour of ten and the doors swung inwards. The small church was almost full, Hattie noticed, though she could not see faces clearly. The local vicar must have gathered his parishioners to support Lord Bentley. She was still in mourning and had hoped for something discreet. Richard escorted her down the aisle, which was full of sunlight shining through the tall stained glass, until she stood next to her future husband in front of the altar. She felt inadequate. It was grossly unfair for him to be so handsome. He wore a dark blue coat of superfine which was tightly fitted to him and her thoughts strayed to what he looked like underneath those elegant clothes. A flush rose in her cheeks as she realized the vicar was speaking and she had not heard a word. She would dearly love to have a fan and to loosen her corset. Edward was watching her with a twinkle in his eye. Could he read her thoughts? How mortifying!

"Do you, Harriet Eleanor Longbottom..."

"Bottom! Bottom!" She heard Archie screech, and the congregation rumbled with suppressed laughter. She looked over to where Lord Bergen stood on the other side of the groom, and there was Archie, with something around his neck, trying to spread his wings.

"What is he doing here?" she whispered.

"We thought you would want him here," Edward whispered back.

She smiled sweetly at him. It *was* very considerate of him. Everyone knew rakes could be charming, though.

"He greeted me as whoremonger," he told her with a wink.

"Oh!"

The vicar cleared his throat in a condemnatory manner and continued with the vows until it was time for her to say, "I will."

What choice did she have, she wondered cynically. When would her wariness cease? She was vowing before God to honor, obey, and cherish a man she did not know.

The time came to exchange rings, and Hattie was surprised. She had played the organ at countless weddings and she knew every note by heart, yet this ceremony was difficult to follow.

Edward took her hand to place the ring on it, and she hoped he could not feel how she shook. He slid a golden band of diamonds and sapphires onto her finger, and it was all she could do not to stare. She had never seen anything so beautiful—certainly she had never owned any such precious gems.

Before she allowed herself to think too much of it, she realized the ring was, in all likelihood, a family heirloom, and a countess was expected to have such extravagance.

"I now pronounce you man and wife."

Before the impact of who she was dawned on her, she was signing her new name in the register and being led back through the chapel. What strange turn of fate had found her now married and a countess to boot?

CHAPTER 7

The ceremony ended and Edward and Hattie immediately walked towards a waiting barouche, ready to take them to their breakfast celebration. Lord Richard Bentley had taken pains to ensure his sister's wedding was flawless. Edward had to admit this was a nice touch. His own coach could have served, but he had not even thought to have it ready at the ceremony's end. Gil, his valet, would use it to make sure his mother arrived at the breakfast.

Holding her hand, he helped his countess into the vehicle. Hattie adjusted her dress and moved to make room for him when he joined her.

"You made a beautiful bride today, Hattie." She truly did look lovely.

"Thank you, my lord." She blushed.

"Edward. I would like it very much if you would call me Edward." He squeezed her hand affectionately.

"Yes, my—Edward." She grinned.

"I have given this a lot of thought, and I found myself...looking forward to our union. I want..." His throat worked as he struggled to find the right words. "I want to have a faithful relationship, despite what our beginning may have led you to believe, and I wanted to tell you that." He had realized, over the past few days, that there was a seed of friendship here, one that he wanted to nurture.

"And that holds for you as well, my lord—the faithfulness?" Her response was direct.

"Yes, Hattie, it does." He glanced about and assured himself that he still had a few minutes before they arrived at her brother's home for their wedding breakfast. He wanted this to be a special moment between the two of them. Reaching into his pocket, he extracted the velvet jewelry pouch. "This is for you." He opened the pouch and pulling out the bracelet, secured it around her gloved wrist.

Hattie gazed down at her wrist. "I have never owned anything so beautiful, Edward. Thank you."

"I am so glad you find it to your liking. The necklace and earrings which match it are inside the pouch. I will hold them if you would like me to."

"I do not know what to say. You have me at a disadvantage, Edward. I have nothing to give you as a gift."

"You do have something I want." He smiled. "Hattie, I realize that the start of our relationship was hardly the way either of us would have chosen, but if you will give me the chance, I will work hard to change your opinion of me. I want this marriage to be a good one." He searched his pocket once more and pulled out a small, carefully wrapped package. "This is also for you."

Hattie unwrapped the thin package and stared at the gift. She looked up at Edward, and picked up the spectacles, holding them close to examine them. "They are finer than the ones I lost, Edward." She carefully placed them on and looked up at him, as her eyes filled with tears. "You did this for me?"

"I saw them in London. When I looked through the lenses, I realized what difficulty you must have seeing without them, and I wanted to change that." He gently regarded her, his forefinger tenderly brushing her chin. "They look nice on you." He kissed her on the cheek. "We have arrived. Here, use this." "He pulled out his pocket linen out and handed it to her. "This might help dry your eyes." Edward watched her dab her eyes with his handkerchief. "Hattie, I hope you will not object to our staying here an extra night or so. I have some business I would like to see finished."

Hattie nodded. "Yes, Edward. I will be happy to stay longer. This gives me a little extra time with my brother, Richard."

"Then it is settled. Shall we greet our guests?" He helped her from the barouche and together they walked through the crowd of cheering friends and family to the banquet hall.

Lord and Lady Bentley met them at the door. "Lord Weston, Lady Weston, welcome!" Her brother hugged her. Edward watched Lady Louisa curtsey to her newly wedded sister-in-law, and held back a chuckle. *I am sure she is enjoying Hattie's new rank.*

"Your seats are this way." Bentley led the bride and groom to their seats. The hall had been transformed with flowers, candles, and tables of food. Ivy wrapped around the round columns and framed tables of desserts—iced cookies and cakes—breads, and meats. A three-tier wedding cake sat in a place of honor on a small table to the right of the round, lace-covered dessert table. Footmen began serving plated food of meats—particularly, duck and pigeon, breads, and vegetables.

"There is so much food, Richard," Hattie offered. "It looks lovely." She reached for her drink and her bracelet dangled, chiming against the glass.

Louisa reached across the table and pulled Hattie's arm to her face. "That looks familiar. Where did you get that bracelet?" Louisa's voice was loud and her tone accusing.

"Louisa, you are mistaken. Please sit down," her disgruntled husband growled. He glared at his wife. "Sit down!" he whispered loudly.

"Jezebel! Too close!" Archie screamed at the back of the exiting woman—presumably, Edward reflected, sensing the need to come to his mistress's rescue. The popinjay flapped his wings loudly.

"Archie, please..." Hattie's reprimand was very weak, hiding behind the broad smile she directed to her bird.

The Dowager Countess seated herself across from Hattie. "I believe, Lady Bentley, that was most probably a gift from my son," she supplied, narrowing her eyes at Louisa.

Edward noticed the sneer on his new sister-in-law's face. The woman did nothing to improve her looks. He thought of lemons—sour ones—each time he glanced at her. Hattie did not look for his help; he could not miss the look of determination on her face. *'Tis best I allow my wife to handle this.* Having decided, he pretended not to hear, and instead concentrated on his plate. His respect for his new wife was growing quickly.

Louisa lightly touched Hattie's arm. "Lord Bentley is correct, my lady. I was just taken with it, as it reminded me of the one my dear departed mother once owned."

Hattie leaned as close to her sister-in-law as she could. She spoke quietly, but firmly.

"Dear Louisa, my sister, should you have such a lapse again, I would beg that you ask me in a place of privacy before you grab my person. Your conduct towards me was most gauche, and I will not respond in kind. My husband presented this bracelet to me this morning on our way here. It is part of his wedding gift to me." She paused. "I will add that you have had more practice at these affairs. I might have looked to you for an example of proper conduct, but, sadly, even I realize that is not to be." She sat back and turned her attention to her plate.

"Well!" Louisa huffed with indignation to the smiling friends and family seated at the table across from her staring her way.

It had been a perfect day, so far, and it was still young. Archie was on a perch, behaving himself; Edward would thank Bergen later. Remarkably for the season, the sun was shining, the weather was crisp, and his wedding had gone off without a hitch, or an acid comment from his mother. He hoped that continued, because the last thing he wanted was a crying bride. He had not overheard the entire exchange, but he thought he had just witnessed his mother defending his new Countess. What could she be about?

The Dowager casually put down her buttered bread. "Lady Weston, I do not believe I have given you a proper greeting. My son should be chastised for hiding such a beautiful bride away from his mother. How did you come to meet my son?"

Lady Louisa nearly choked on her wine. "You mean you have not heard? They were caught..."

Eyes turned towards the newly wedded couple.

"I believe Lady Weston was speaking to me, dear sister." Hattie cut Lady Bentley off in mid-sentence. She placed her wine glass down and adjusted her glasses on her face. "Oh dear. I believe you have..." She gestured demurely to her sister in law. "Yes, now that I see it better, I believe it is yellow pollen from the irises in the vase, here, on your face. Perhaps you got too close to the blooms. Mayhap you should go to the retiring room to remove it? I should hate for it to be brushed into your eye by accident." She smiled sweetly. Her lips still curved, she watched Louisa leave the room in a barely concealed temper.

"My lady," she addressed Edward's mother, "I believe you were asking how we met?"

Edward looked at his wife with renewed respect. He had been ready to intervene at his mother's question, but when Hattie had squeezed his hand, he had stopped. He had not married a shrinking violet. He glanced down and saw that his wife's hand was trembling slightly in her lap, the only sign of her fear. Even so, she had managed to rebuke her disagreeable sister-in-law, twice, and with kindness. It occurred to him that now would be a good time to rescue her. He cleared his throat, drawing the attention of everyone around him.

"Mother, we met by chance at a posting house. I noticed her as soon as I arrived." He had seen her, but it had taken drink and fate to awaken him to her special qualities. He smiled at his mother, waiting for any further questions. She merely nodded in their direction, a peculiar expression on her face.

Bentley smiled and nodded, clearly pleased with his response.

Oddly, his mother was still beaming with pride and looking directly at his wife. "My dear, I believe we will become great friends. I think this could have been the first thing—" She smiled up at her son. "—he and I have agreed upon in an age!"

"Thank you, Mother, I think." He smiled. "I look forward to that."

Hattie was no longer showing any outward signs of nerves. Had he died and gone to heaven where he had a mother who could possibly like his wife, and perhaps, one day, like him a little too? Edward considered his luck as he took a large sip from his glass of wine.

A footman finished serving champagne to all the guests, ending with Bergen.

"A toast!" he cried, standing, his glass elevated. "A toast to my best friend and his new bride. May each day bring you closer and may your marriage be long and prosperous."

"Hear, hear!" Collective voices resounded.

"May I offer a toast?"

Edward's mother also rose to her feet, startling him yet again. Unsure of what to say or anticipate, he nodded.

"To my son and my new daughter-in-law. May you find all you need in this life from each other." She smiled and gave a slight nod in his direction before sitting down again.

"Hear, hear!" The table of voices chanted back.

"Hear, hear!" asserted Archie shrilly. Everyone broke into laughter, including Edward's mother and his new bride. The bird flapped; it seemed to be his way to say he was pleased with himself.

Edward gazed at his mother. She seemed well. But was this the same woman he had spoken with just a day ago? He wrestled with his thoughts, unsure of what to think. His eyes sought out his friend, and noticed he had been watching. Bergen merely shrugged.

"Edward." Hattie's quiet voice drew his attention. "I need to be excused to the retiring room. I will be back, husband." She smiled at him as she withdrew from the table.

Edward watched his wife leave, and then gazed in his mother's direction, catching a smile from her. *Perhaps this is her idea of a truce.* If so, he would take it. He reached for a fresh glass of wine from the footman. In his estimation, this day was only going to get better. He nodded to Bergen, and took another sip of wine, feeling optimistic for the first time in a while.

Hattie had smiled and greeted more titled people that day then she had ever met, collectively. Everyone was suddenly deferential and calling her 'lady.' These gatherings were much more sophisticated than such events in her village. Being a countess was exhausting. She would happily return to being Hattie Longbottom and live alone in the cottage in Little Whitley. She was grateful to have spectacles once again. That had been a most considerate and surprising gift from her new husband. *Husband.* What a strange feeling, to think she was forever bound to this man when she had resolved to be a spinster. It gave her the most pressing headache. Perhaps a few moments' rest would not be noticed. Whispering her intent to Weston, she escaped from the ballroom and was walking toward the staircase when she overheard voices arguing.

"Philip, what are you doing here? You are not known to these people and after that disastrous duel a year ago, I thought we had agreed..."

"Dear sister, do not portend to lecture me. I need funds. I came to get them from you. I seem to find myself momentarily short of the ready. No one is paying me."

"You mean your blackmail scheme has failed? You *killed* a man. His friends—" She lowered her voice. "—are here. You told me how angry you were that he had not believed the debts you made up. You should leave, before someone recognizes you and connects it to things they have heard about others! Find another way to cover your debts."

"What would you know of the matter? My funds have been covering your gambling habit. You are as much a part of this as I am."

"No! I never told you to seek revenge on..."

"Silence! You will not say another word. I will tell you the way of it, sister. If you do not get me five thousand pounds I will share your gambling habit with your dear husband."

"No, you will not."

"Yes, I most certainly will. And you will get the money for me because if you make your husband aware of my misdeed, I will point to him as the one who killed that man."

"You cannot. You were seen."

"By a spineless coward. I took care of him. He will never say anything."

The woman shrieked, "You killed another?"

A slap echoed in the hallway and Hattie decided to move to safety. She was not sure what this was about, but she knew it was something bad... and her brother could be hurt by it.

She gasped. When had her sister-in-law turned in to such a wretched human being? Although it was true she had not had many dealings with Louisa, there had been a time when she had thought her tolerable, if not amiable. Now, she could only see her as selfish and cruel. Poor Richard! Did he have any idea? Should she tell him, or should she mind her own business?

Mayhap Weston could advise her. He was her husband, after all. She would try to determine what she should do later, but for now she must lie down. She walked to her chamber instead of the retiring room and decided a few moments on the settee would ease the pain in her head.

Hattie felt she must be having her special dream again, the one where the handsome stranger came to sweep her off her feet and carry her away to a new life. The difference, this time, was that it was her handsome husband's face she saw. She tried not to fight the dream, telling herself she was now married and these activities would be necessary. The sensations she felt were strange; she could not yet decide whether or not they were pleasurable. He was whispering endearments into her ear, his warm breath making her shiver. As he showered tender kisses upon her neck and face, her arms slipped wantonly over her head to allow him greater access to her body. The invitation was accepted, and his warm hands began to roam all over her. Hattie heard a moan and realized it came from her own lips as her husband began to caress her in tender places. Her body writhed of its own accord, seeking she knew not what, and she was filled with a longing for something she could not name.

"Yes, that's my girl. Let yourself relax," he encouraged.

"Oh..." She moaned as his hand slid, inch by teasing inch, down over her abdomen and lower... She woke up fully and started at his intimate touch.

"Shh. It is only I, my dear. Do not fight it. And please, do not beat my... snake with a pillow!" He laughed.

"I did not know before," she whimpered.

"You were, nevertheless, enjoying my ministrations."

She was now, as well, and she blushed with the knowledge. He was exploring places she hardly dared touch herself, save when bathing.

"Close your eyes and allow it to happen, Hattie. I will not harm you."

"I know," she whispered, willing herself to calm down and stop trembling.

Allow it to happen. Sally had said the same, earlier.

He lifted her from the settee and began to unbutton her gown. She must have fallen into a deep sleep. Passively, she allowed him to slide the garment down her body. She wished she could have stayed safely dreaming for a bit longer. Now she was self-conscious about what he would think of her, and what was to come. No doubt there had been scores of other women, if Louisa's hurtful remarks were to be believed, and now, on her wedding day, Hattie could only think of how unsatisfactory a lover she would be. Picking her up, Edward carried her across the room to place her on the bed. She could feel the strength in his arms and thighs, the muscled breadth of his chest and the firmness of... She swallowed, certain that part of him would not fit where God ordained it should. He came down beside her, the feel of his skin warm against hers. Her stomach turned a somersault.

"Edward?"

"Mm?" The murmur had a questioning note as, with lips, tongue, and fingers, he stroked and teased her flesh. It was decidedly difficult to think when he did such things.

"How is this going to work?" She realized she had asked an inappropriate question by the look of abject horror which crossed his face. He blinked twice and then relaxed.

"Do you know nothing about what happens between a man and a woman?"

"A little," she answered shyly. "I know your..." she waved downward... "joins with me." She swallowed again. Why had she asked? He must think her an unsophisticated simpleton, but she could not help it.

A look of tenderness crossed his face and he pulled himself up to lie on his side next to her, though he continued to caress her.

"I should have asked you first. I did not think properly when I saw you lying on the settee... I wanted to make you my wife."

He wanted her? It was a shocking thought.

"I will slow down and prepare you for me. It will fit and it will feel good to you—at least after the first time."

"I believe you." And she did. He was being very kind and patient with her, for which she was grateful. It could have been very different.

"Hattie?"

"Yes?"

"You can touch me, too. In fact, I would rather you participated. The physical side of marriage can be wonderfully pleasurable for both of us."

Hattie could scarcely believe what she was hearing.

"Not only harlots and whoremongers are allowed to enjoy this." He laughed seductively in her ear as his hand explored further.

She jumped when he reached her most intimate place; a shock of sensation swept through her body. It was hard not to giggle.

"Does that feel nice?" he asked, circling his tongue around her ear.

"Yes," she replied breathlessly.

"Put your hands on me. Touch me, explore me; know me, my wife.

She could barely concentrate, given what his hands were doing to her body, but she placed her own, trembling, hand upon his chest. It was difficult to lie still for the sensations spreading through her body. Her hand grew bold and began to explore his hard, muscular chest and abdomen. The fine hair was like nothing she had ever felt and she teased it through her fingers. She continued downward; the hair grew thicker and she found the part of him which was supposed to join him to her. Suddenly, she knew a longing to feel, to understand; she became dizzy with the very thought.

Boldly, she placed her hand on him, slowly turning herself towards his embrace.

She heard him laughing as though through a tunnel. Heat coursed along her veins and over her skin as he continued to touch her.

"I agree. I think you are ready," he said, supporting himself on his arms above her.

Tension shot through her body as she felt him enter her. She gasped at the pressure.

"You must relax now," he gently commanded. "It will pass."

After a moment, the discomfort eased and as he continued to kiss her, she felt him fill her completely. It was like nothing she had ever felt before. Strange pulsations began to sweep through her body, and she felt pleasure previously unknown to her. Then he began to move within her and she held onto his body, wanting him closer. A storm began to grow inside her; a tempest of emotion which exploded in an intense series of spasms that swarmed her senses until she felt her consciousness fading.

When she came to, a warm arm and leg were draped over her naked body. She turned to see Edward watching her.

It was hard not to panic, and she began fumbling for something with which to cover herself. His hand reached out to stop her.

"Hattie."

She froze.

"No. Why do you wish to hide from me?"

"I—am unused to baring myself, my lord."

"Come." He stood, confident in his full, naked glory, and held his hand out to her. She took it, though she held her other hand to cover herself as much as possible. Taking her spectacles from the side-table, he placed them gently on her nose before leading her to the looking-glass. He stood behind her and she thought she must die of mortification. Never before had she looked at herself thus.

"Please do not make me do this. I know I am not what you are used to."

"You are correct." He took his hand and pulled her hair to the side and traced his lips over her neck. "You are much more beautiful."

She swallowed nervously and watched him lazily watching her in the glass while he began to touch her all over again. His voice sent shivers down her body when he whispered how perfect was every part of her, whilst caressing each place. Soon, her body was on fire and her legs were trembling. She was certain she would swoon if he continued.

"I want you to see what I see, Hattie."

When he touched her like that, she doubted she would see much for long. Fortunately, he was merciful and led her back to the bed for further explorations into the realms of marital bliss.

CHAPTER 8

The sun sliced through the heavy pink curtains, waking Edward. He turned to look at his wife, still sleeping beside him, her arm draped over his chest. He lifted the thick velour cover slightly and took in the sight of her—which created an immediate longing. Her eyes fluttered open and the corner of her mouth drew up in a slight smile. He never would have guessed the indignant spinster from the inn would have turned out to be so...voracious in bed.

He noticed she did not move away from him. "You are awake, Lady Weston." He rose over her and looked into her eyes. "Are you hungry, wife?" His eyes glinted mischievously.

"Yes, but...uh...I have an even stronger craving, one that is new to me," she confessed, she squeezed her eyes almost shut, against a wave of sudden shyness.

"I think I know what the lady needs." His voice was low and seductive. "My lady wife, you are full of surprises. I think I am going to enjoy being leg-shackled to you." Slowly, he pulled the covers over his head and began sprinkling kisses down her throat and on, lower, towards her most intimate place.

"Edward...it is morning."

"And a very beautiful one indeed. Let us not waste a moment of it."

EARL OF WESTON

A loud scuffling noise in the hall roused them both away from their pleasure.

"I do not know when I have had such an energetic night...and morning...and still, I have managed to wake so refreshed." He folded his arms behind his head and looked up at the ceiling, seeing nothing, really. It felt good. "We should probably dress and go down to break our fast. I find that I do not want to leave the bed." Last night, and this morning—it had been more than he had anticipated. His little wife was completely different in the bedroom. *She had probably surprised herself,* he thought, smiling. "You do not mind if I refer to our pleasuring each other, do you, wife?"

"Edward..." She seemed impatient to tell him something. "Edward, would you mind terribly if we talked *before* we get dressed? I heard something upsetting and feel that I should tell you."

"Did my mother say something? Please, just tell me and..." He knew he should have been more protective towards Hattie in the presence of his mother.

She interrupted him. "No, Edward, it was not your mother. She has actually been most gracious to me. We chatted for only a few moments yesterday, but I am hopeful she will spend some time with us." She sighed loudly.

"What is it, my dearest?" He realized he had just called her dearest. It surprised him, but he did feel comfortable with her, with this—and with more. Nevertheless, he was not ready to reflect on those thoughts. He would rather just enjoy.

"I fear you may become angry when I tell you, but I am so confused over it."

"Now you have me concerned." He propped himself up on one arm and faced her. When this overwhelming feeling of protectiveness had begun, he could not be sure, but he did not want anyone to harm even her feelings. He needed to let her talk. It was a lesson he had learned, and learned well, while working with the Crown.

"I was tired and thought to go to my chambers to take a brief nap."

"Yes, I recall. You left early, so I followed shortly after." He noticed her uneasiness.

"Before you found me here, Edward, I passed Louisa's parlor and heard arguing."

"Go on," he urged, softly.

"It was Louisa and her brother, Mr. Martin. They were arguing angrily. She was talking about a duel that he attended, and how his had killed a man. He told her to keep quiet or he would be forced to involve my brother—and implicate him..."

"Wait. This duel, did they give any more specific details?" He felt sick to his stomach. Could it be possible that Martin was involved? *There was the note Mother had given me. That was signed, 'Martin.' Could there be a connection, here?*

"Yes. I think they said it was almost a year ago." She looked up at him, her eyes brimming with tears. "Do you think this could have anything to do with—" she started, but stopped. "Could it involve my brother?" Her lower lip trembled.

"I do not know, but I plan to find out. Soon." He felt his anger welling up, but it had nothing to do with Hattie and everything to do with Mr. Martin. Surely it could not involve Lord Bentley as well? Edward realized he had to gain a better perspective, and be calmer, for Hattie. He shuddered to think of a friend being responsible for his brother's death. Edward was almost sure this information was the piece of the puzzle he had been looking for all this time. He sensed this was the very same duel, which had taken his brother's life. He wanted to read the note again, but he did not have it with him. He could ask his mother. *Mayhap Mother knows more than she realizes.* He had to know the connection to Robert. For the nonce, he needed Bergen.

"Hattie, do you recall anything else?"

"He said he had taken care of someone else and Louisa screamed at him, asking if he had killed another. A noise almost gave me away, so I did not hear anything else." She said the words slowly.

"I did not give you much opportunity to tell me this last night." He addressed Hattie softly. "Wife, you have surprised me in more ways than one." His voice fell to a whisper and he regarded her with gravity. "I am anxious to learn all there is to know about you as we grow old together, yet can I ask you to keep this information to yourself? Until I find out more about the matter, we need to keep this quiet." A chilling thought stopped him. "They did not see you, did they?"

"No. They were not paying any attention. Louisa said he needed to find another source for money since his blackmail scheme had failed, and that it was too dangerous for him to be seen here amongst friends of the man he had killed. He threatened to implicate my brother if she did not cooperate! They argued some more, and I heard her slap him, so I slipped away to our chamber. I worried how I could ask you about it until my head hurt. The next thing I knew, you had become my dream."

"Well, that is the first time a woman has ever given me such a compliment, my dearest." He smiled warmly at her, before his voice took on a somber tone. "Hattie, my brother was important to me. On the last occasion we talked, we argued about my debts. I treated him badly..."

"So, you are carrying guilt over his death," she offered, her tone sympathetic.

"Yes, mainly because I knew something and did not disclose it—his betrothed was unfaithful to him. I was angry and I behaved selfishly. Had I told him, I might have kept him from finding out in the way he did and, as a result, dying in a duel." He had just shared something he had not intended. It was so easy to talk to her. "Hattie, I must ask that you do not speak of this to anyone else."

"Not even to your mother?"

"Especially not to my mother."

"She cares for you, Edward."

"I do not want to discuss her right now." He quieted her with a kiss. "We must get dressed. Let us break our fast together."

He appreciated that Bentley had allocated them a suite of rooms. He would go to his and ring for Gil. "I shall be back at half-past, my dear."

She nodded, smiling. "I will take a bath. I think the warm water will do me good."

He leaned over and kissed her cheek. "Hattie, one more thing I feel the need to share. I confess, with you I find myself more open than I have ever been, and truly, that scares me. So, I must ask again, for your promise to keep this just between the two of us."

"Edward, I promise."

"I believe you. It is about Robert's death. You are speaking with Mother and I know that she believes I was engaged in my old activities at the time of Robert's death..."

She nodded, yet remained quiet.

"I was not. I was working."

"Working? I am confused, husband. You have an...occupation?"

"Well, yes and no." He smiled at her lack of guile. "I have been an agent of the Crown. I was... although I am so no more. Robert died, and..."

"And you had to come home." She finished the sentence for him.

"Yes. I was not here. As much as I wish I had been, I cannot change that."

"I understand, Edward."

"Thank you." He squeezed her hand, kissed her cheek and then headed to his own bedchamber.

Edward had some business to attend to, so Hattie decided to visit Archie and take him to the orangery. He had hopped up and down in delight to see her again and was equally ecstatic to fly around amongst the trees and flowers in the large, bright room despite the threatening sky outside. Hattie could not stop worrying about the argument she had overheard and how it would affect her brother—and perhaps her husband. Edward had been very concerned by what she had told him, and she had wanted to wipe his anxieties away. She had discovered an unexpected affection for her husband already, in more ways than one. Warmth from deep inside swept over her when she recalled precisely how they had spent several hours of their first day as man and wife. He had surprised her with his consideration and she found she was hopeful for the future. She strolled among the exotic plants while

Archie flitted about overhead, the wheels in her mind turning furiously to find a way she could help her husband.

Hattie plucked a flower and fidgeted with the pink petals as she cogitated what to do. Perhaps she could confront Louisa or Mr. Martin herself? Yet, how could she protect her brother? Her new husband was clearly pained by his own brother's death, and she hoped to save him more heartache, if at all possible. The problem was, she did not know how to convince Louisa or Mr. Martin. She had never dealt with anyone of their ilk. Pleading to their sense of goodness or honour was unlikely to move them.

"What are you fretting over, child?" A lady's voice called to her.

Hattie started and turned to find the source of the question. She discovered her new mother-in-law resting in a chair, in the corner with a view over the wide park with woodland beyond.

"My apologies. I did not see you there, my lady."

"It is always wise to search your surroundings at a house party," she advised. "You never know what you might happen upon at these things. Now, come sit by me and tell me what troubles you."

Hattie sat down obediently, but was afraid to pour her heart out when her husband had strictly forbidden it.

"Are you afraid to tell me? I know more than you might give me credit for," Lady Weston said wryly.

"Oh, no, I... it is merely that Weston asked me not to speak to anyone about it."

"Even me?" She waved her hand. "Do not answer. I am sure he said *especially* me."

"He did not wish to worry you," Hattie reassured her.

"He does not wish me to meddle," her ladyship corrected. "I do hope he will put himself on the straight and narrow now that he has married."

"Was he so very wild?" Hattie asked.

"No more than most boys his age with no prospects for a title, I expect. Many young men sow their oats, but what pains me most is his brother died while trying to help him. Edward was gallivanting in Paris, when Robert was killed in a duel."

"Edward mentioned he had made some poor choices." Hattie frowned as the Dowager grunted her agreement in an unladylike fashion. "However, he was not gallivanting. I hope in time he will tell you what he was doing, for I think you would be proud of him." She shifted uncomfortably, hoping she had not said too much.

"I beg your pardon?" The Dowager regarded her with so much hope, and at the same time with so much pain and sadness, that Hattie could not bear it. "Please, Hattie. Tell me the whole of it, for it is long past time my son and I reconciled. I have already lost one son. I cannot lose another... and I fear greatly that I have."

Hattie could not find it in her heart to refuse Edward's mother. Married just a day, and she was about to betray her husband's trust. She felt sick.

She shook her head. "He will be angry with me."

"Then he need not find out, need he? You were trying to think of how to help him, were you not? Perhaps I may lend my assistance. I know these people much better than you do. If I have wronged my son, then let me help to make amends. If it is any consolation, I probably have most of the information already, but just have not put it together properly. So you would not really be revealing secrets."

What Lady Weston said was true. And Hattie did want to help Edward. She sighed. "I can tell you what I know. I overheard Lady Louisa and Mr. Martin arguing as I went to rest last evening. Mr. Martin seemed to be making threats towards Louisa about my poor brother and I was anxious, but when I told Edward about it, he was more concerned about the duel they had also mentioned."

"I do wonder..." the Dowager said, appearing to be thinking. "I found a letter in Robert's effects. It was signed by a Martin."

"Is it of significance, do you think?"

"Perhaps it is. I wish I could recall the precise words, but it was requesting payment for Edward's gambling debts, the week before the wretched duel."

"It has to be the same Martin!" Hattie exclaimed. "This must be what Edward surmised when I told him of the argument. He said he had unfinished business to deal with before we could leave. I must tell Richard if his wife and brother-in-law are involved in gambling schemes and duels. If Mr. Martin is desperate for funds, he will doubtless attempt to extract them from someone."

"Edward will need to pay if they are, in fact, his debts."

"Something in this does not make sense. Edward mentioned he was away when his brother died. How could he have gambling debts to Mr. Martin if he was away?"

"Wait one moment. Perhaps we should arrange the matter ourselves," the Dowager suggested with a gleam in her eye. "If he was attempting to cheat money from Robert, he will have no qualms about trying the same tactics on Edward."

"What can we do?"

"I need to consider. Perhaps after my afternoon nap, I might have an answer. Pray Edward and Bergen do not do anything imprudent before I think of something." The Dowager stood to leave and Hattie called Archie back to her.

Archie nestled on her shoulder, making his purring sound in her ear, as she decided a walk would refresh her and give her time to think of her own plan. Taking an umbrella from the stand by the door, she made her way across the terrace and down the steps through the parterre garden. There was no formal walking path, but Hattie decided to head towards the lake which lay beyond the wide expanse of open field.

"It looks the perfect distance, Archie. What say you?"

"Pretty boy, pretty boy."

"I think so, too. Now, we must think of a way to help Edward and Richard," she said to the bird. He put his head on one side; he was used to listening to her discourse about her problems or worries. "However, Mr. Martin is not a nice man. He was threatening to blackmail his own sister last night, so how can we keep him away from our dear Edward?"

"Whoremonger! Whoremonger!"

"Yes, dear, but we must find another name for you to call him," she said in a stern voice as she rounded a hedge and almost bumped into a privy which stood beside a gardener's shed. She was about to turn and walk away from it when she heard arguing again.

She recognized the voices. Why was she forever overhearing Louisa and her brother, and in the most precarious of all places? Hattie knew she had to listen in. She held her nose and crept inside the privy, moving to the only knot-hole she could find and tried to look out. She whispered "shh" to Archie, praying the furtive pair did not discover her here, and her feathered guardian kept quiet.

"This is all I could obtain, Philip," Louisa said angrily as she shoved something into his hands.

"It is a start, certainly," he said in a musing tone. He ran a diamond bracelet through his fingers. "If you include the set, it might hold the creditors at bay, at least temporarily."

"No! There will be no more, Philip. You must find another way. You will ruin my marriage!"

"You should have thought of that before losing your head at the faro tables, Louisa. Your losses rival those of the Duchess of Devonshire."

"Be that as it may, I have reformed my ways. There can be no more left to repay. I have been bled dry!" She crossed her arms and stamped her foot.

"Interest, dear sister. Interest. You are fortunate I have managed this for you."

"Humph. What if Hampton decides to squeak? He may be as tired as I of paying. I saw Weston questioning him before you arrived. Hampton looked decidedly uncomfortable—and is now nowhere to be found."

"Do you think Weston suspects?" he asked. There was a very concerned look upon his face.

"I am sure I do not know, brother. I think it best if you leave as soon as possible and rusticate for a while."

Louisa took his arm, as if to lead him away that very moment. He jerked out of her hold.

"Not so fast. I need to discover what Weston knows."

"You cannot murder everyone who might know something, Philip!

Hampton, Perry, Bergen...one peer is more than sufficient. They will make the connections quickly enough if you dispose of anyone else," she growled at him angrily. "Now you must leave!"

Hattie thought they would never stop talking. Now she needed them to hurry on. She was growing weary of being closeted in the outhouse, and did not know how much longer Archie would be quiet.

"Perhaps you are correct. You go on ahead. I will gather my belongings and be out of your way today," he said, clearly offended.

"I do wish you well, brother, contrary to how this appears. I wish the situation were otherwise." She kissed him on the cheek before hurrying away.

"Jezebel!" Archie crowed.

"Hush!" Hattie reprimanded and prayed Mr. Martin had walked out of earshot. He had not.

"Who is there?" he demanded, banging on the door. "Come out at once!"

Frantically, Hattie tried to think of a plan. She did not want this man to get away and kill Edward, but she had to manage to keep herself alive. Trembling, she unlatched the door and stepped out, grateful for the fresh air.

"Good day to you, Mr. Martin. I apologize for monopolizing the privy. It is all yours." She smiled in what she hoped was a foolish manner and tried to step away, while thinking feverishly of how to trap him.

"You are not going anywhere, Lady Weston." He lunged forward and tried to grab her arm.

"Murderer! Murderer!" Archie shrieked and began to flap and peck at Martin.

CHAPTER 9

Good day, my lord! Welcome to the Red Lion. "May I take your coat and cane, my lord?"

"Yes, thank you. I am meeting Lord Bergen."

"Very good, my lord. His lordship is waiting for you in the taproom. This way." The landlord nodded to one of his underlings, who led Edward to the taproom.

Bergen was perusing a newspaper and sipping a brandy when Edward walked into the low-beamed room.

"Weston! You look well. I had not considered that we would be spending time together just one day after the vows." He flashed a grin. "This is a nice place. I did not realize such delightful accommodations existed here in Eynsham. However, I doubt screaming parrots would be welcome." He pointed to the seat across from him. A snifter of amber liquid sat waiting on the walnut table. "I took the liberty of ordering you a brandy. I conjectured it must be important."

"It definitely is, or I would not have interrupted my wedded bliss to spend time with you." Edward stared at the window, without seeing it. After a moment, he swung his gaze back to the room. "Bergen, I think I may know who killed Robert."

"How did you accomplish this? You were married only yesterday and in that space of time you have discovered the identity of the person responsible for your brother's death? That is not the usual post-wedding activity, my friend." He frowned and put down his brandy. "You have my complete attention."

"Hattie overheard an argument and she shared the details with me this morning."

"You think someone who attended your wedding killed your brother?"

"I think it is highly possible." He leaned forward. "Mr. Philip Martin—you recall his late arrival at the house party, do you not? He is brother to Louisa, Lady Bentley."

"Yes...and from everything I have heard about him lately, he is a blackguard. He is someone to avoid. Nonetheless, it will take some convincing for me to believe Lord and Lady Bentley were connected to anything to do with Robert's death."

"I confess I am not sure of their involvement. I have reason to believe it is possible. My wife—" His blood quickened when he mentioned Hattie. "—was heading to her bedchamber when she over-heard Mr. Martin and his sister arguing loudly. She said she heard them discuss the duel, and the death of a person involved in the duel —although they did not name him, I believe it to be Robert. She told me Lady Louisa referred to the time which had elapsed as being less than a year, and also that the person killed had friends at the house party. It is puzzling. Yet my instinct tells me it is the same duel."

Bergen reflected for a second or two. "There *are* rumors of his pockets being to let, as well as reports of extortion."

"I had not heard those, but it fits with the rest." Edward rubbed his forehead in frustration.

"You could be right. I would not have thought of him." Bergen reached for his brandy. "He is a vindictive chap, or so I have heard from people who have crossed him. Still, I would not have thought him capable of murder."

"Perhaps it was an accident. I do not know, but I doubt that. Barring an eyewitness or confession, we will have a difficult time proving his involvement. He did not confess to anything specific.

Most likely, I will have to force a confession—unless a witness comes forward or can be discovered. It appears Hampton is also connected somehow, although thus far he has avoided me. Hattie said she was told he left in a hurry. Hampton's behavior is entirely strange, do you not think?"

"Let us not get ahead of ourselves, Weston. I am having trouble believing that your new relatives could possibly be connected to your brother's death. Besides, I am fascinated at the closeness you and your new bride have found together."

"We rub along tolerably well, it seems."

"Yes, I can see that you do." Bergen allowed his smile to stretch across his face.

"Do be serious!" Edward regretted his burst of temper. He wanted Bergen to concentrate on Robert, not his marriage. "There is more. I have a letter that Martin penned to Robert. When I saw Mother before my wedding, she passed it to me. She said it was in Robert's possessions. She did not see it to be of any significance, but I think he tried to extort money from my brother. He claims he is owed for vowels of mine, accumulated during the week before the duel." He pushed the note across the table and waited for Bergen to read it.

Edward glowered at the bent head.

"Not only have I always settled my debts or gone to Robert myself, but I was in Paris, working. Robert knew this and I believe he refused to meet the man; either that or, perhaps, he threatened to have him arrested."

Bergen finished reading the note and leaned back in his chair. "I agree. This fits with your extortion theory. With what Hattie reported, it points to Martin's involvement." He studied his drink. "There is no chance anyone saw Hattie when she overheard this, was there?"

"I hope not. She did not think so." His throat felt dry despite the refreshment. "I have left her at the house, but Mother is there, as well." He felt better knowing she was not alone. "They seem to be affable towards one another, strange as that seems."

"And Archie..."

"Yes. The popinjay is there, too. No doubt that limits her activity." He furrowed his brow. "Now that I consider it, I recall Perry, Hampton's brother, complaining that Hampton had been driven out of Town, but he refused to be specific."

"I have been thinking about that. What hold could Martin have over Hampton? The man has always been above reproach." He laughed. "He is rather boring."

"I could not say. Hampton has known our family all his life. Robert was his best friend. Why will he not meet with me? If he needs help, I would hope that he would feel he could talk with me."

Bergen lowered his voice. "I think we need to talk to Hampton. We can use him to lure Martin out and possibly get him to confess."

"That is a good idea, only our bait has gone."

"Well, not exactly. A certain...lady...told me that Hampton is here."

For the first time in what seemed an eternity, Edward felt real hope. He knew Hampton was key, but could not know exactly how. Could Hampton have seen something related to Martin and Robert?

"Hampton is here, at the Red Lion?"

Bergen nodded.

"Well, let us find him." Rising, they both went in search of the innkeeper.

"My good man," Bergen addressed the innkeeper, "we are in town for a wedding and the groom is staying here, upstairs. We would like to show him a good time before his big day." He winked.

"That is very odd, my lord. We would have heard if we were having a wedding. What is your friend's name?"

"Lord Hampton. And I believe the wedding is just a small family affair to be held at a small chapel down the road. We are surprising him. Do you know if he is in his room at the moment? We would like to surprise him. He is a little nervous about the big day," Edward added, feeling as if he had fallen back in time to his days at Eton, where he and Bergen had always been playing pranks on the other boys.

"My lords, I should not do this, but I enjoy a good prank and I can see no harm in it." The man glanced around him, presumably to ensure they were not overheard. "He is in the room at the end of the hall. That way." He pointed to the stairs beside his desk.

"Thank you."

"Keep this for your trouble." Edward handed the innkeeper a gold sovereign and they hurried towards the staircase. "Wait." he added, pausing with one booted foot on the bottom step. "We need a plan."

"Weston, it is simple. We tell Hampton we know his secret, and we are going to help him with Martin."

"Ah. As long as we can follow our plan it might work." Edward fairly flew up the steps, taking them two at a time, with Bergen following close behind. Edward knocked on Hampton's door and they waited.

The wooden door opened and Hampton stood looking at the two of them, his mouth agape.

"I do not need anything from either of you." He looked at Bergen angrily and started to close the door.

"Wait." Edward wedged his foot in the doorway. "This is about Robert. We know about Martin blackmailing you." *As they say, in for a penny, in for a pound.*

"You do?" Hampton gave an incredulous look. He looked down the hall, and then back at them.. "Come in."

Twenty minutes later, the three of them were riding towards the Bentley estate. Edward turned in his saddle to regard his companions.

"We are betting on a note from Hampton luring Martin to the stables. Bergen, would you mind delivering the note to the house? Rejoin us as quickly as possible. I doubt Martin will think anything of it if he sees you at the door and, in all probability, will assume I am still with Hattie." He noticed beads of sweat above Hampton's brow. There was more to this than gambling debts. "Hampton," he continued, "I appreciate your helping us. You confirmed that this man killed my brother. I want him. The magistrate has agreed to meet us. Stay out of sight, now, until we have him."

"I will."

$\sim$

"Get the damn bird away from me or he will soon adorn some lady's headdress!" Mr. Martin shouted at Hattie. He reminded her of her handy hat pin, so she slipped it from her bonnet and held it in her hand in case.

"How dare you threaten my Archie!" she screamed in outrage, momentarily emboldened by having her umbrella and a hat pin to use as weapons. It was clear this man was a menace and needed to be dealt with quickly. Unfortunately, her lessons had never included training in battle, and her knight in shining armor was nowhere to be seen, let alone riding ventre-à-terre to the rescue. He was away on Crown business.

She was quite used to saving herself in her spinster dreams; it was when she awoke from them she realized there was no actual knight. Now that she did have one, it would have been lovely to have been rescued.

"It is you and me, Archie," Hattie said softly as she waved her weapons at the horrid man and tried to run towards the gardener's shed. In there, she hoped she might find a sturdier weapon with which to defend herself. She was too far away from the house for anyone to hear her shouts, and so far, she'd been unable to get past him.

"You are mad," Mr. Martin sneered, cutting her off once more while also attempting to fend off the bird's pecking. "I will be doing Weston a favor, helping to rid him of an unwanted wife. I am afraid you now know too much for me to let you live."

"Murderer! Murderer!" Archie squawked.

Hattie saw the man reaching for something in his coat and lunged at him with her hat pin.

"Archie, fly home! Get help!" she commanded. The bird obeyed and flew away.

"You witch!" he screamed, striking her with the back of his hand as she stuck the long pin into his arm. The force of the blow caused her to drop her umbrella. Undaunted, she tried to wrestle his weapon away from him. Her beloved new spectacles flew to the ground in the mêlée. The man might look a dandy, but he was rather strong. Could she lure him backwards into the privy and trap him? It was hard to think while struggling with the man over his knife, but she did manage to recall it latched from inside. The shed was a better option since it locked outwardly, she decided quickly. She let go of the arm which held the knife and ran the few paces to the shed, pausing by the open door as he ran after her. At the last second, as he attempted to swing the knife at her, she leaped aside. He fell into the shed, but managed to catch her leg and drag her in with him. She scrambled to her feet and grabbed a sturdy garden shovel with which to defend herself as the knife went skating across the floor.

He also attempted to scramble to his feet and reclaim the blade, but she struck him in the chest with the shovel, causing him to stagger. But she had not hit him hard enough to knock him out and escape. He'd grabbed a garden hoe and now blocked the doorway. What was she to do now?

He laughed, condescension dripping from every sound. "Did you really think to hold me here with that flimsy weapon until someone comes to rescue you? Or do you believe you can get the better of me with it?"

A peal of thunder clapped through the air, shaking the ground. The wind began to howl and, in the same breath, slammed the door shut.

"Drat!" Hattie muttered as she realized there was no hope for escape now. They were locked in.

He laughed again. "Have you just now realized you are trapped, Miss Longbottom? Forgive me, I mean, your ladyship," he mocked.

"I do realize you seem to enjoy murderous pursuits. However, the shed locks from the outside, so we are both quite trapped in here until someone chooses to release us," she snapped, still holding tight to her sturdy shovel.

"Do you think a simple latch will deter me?" He took a step toward her, but she swung her weapon at him in warning, managing to strike him on the wrist. "Bollocks!"

"Sir!" She reprimanded his language without thinking and for an instant he managed to flush.

"Save your self-righteousness for someone who cares," he snarled. "By the time your dear husband finds us, you will have met with a terrible mishap and I was unable to go for help. They will find me most distressed."

She held her ground, holding tightly to the shovel as heavy rain began to pour on the roof of the small shed. She scanned the enclosure, making note of other garden tools that could be used as weapons in case he should try to pull the shovel from her grasp.

They stood there for some minutes. He continued to look amused while she steadfastly stood her ground, scowling fiercely at him. She was uncertain how long she would be required to hold him at bay until someone found them there, but she refused to let him murder her and escape, or attempt to murder her Edward.

She tried not to let her thoughts wander as her arm grew tired from holding the heavy instrument. Biting her lip, she swung the shovel at him with renewed vigor whenever he attempted to approach, determined to see the adventure to its conclusion. Someone would have to miss them before long, would they not? She began to doubt.

"No one will willingly come out in the storm, Lady Weston," he taunted as though he had read her thoughts.

"Mayhap they will not, but I will not willingly allow you to murder my husband as you did his brother!"

"You believe you are clever, but I am growing bored. There is no proof of your accusations, true though they may be. It will be your word against mine."

"Stay back," she commanded when he attempted to lunge at her to end their standoff. He grabbed for the handle of the shovel and tried to wrestle it from her hands. She managed to hold him off by rapping him on the knuckles with it.

"Ouch!" He sucked at the knuckles she had just hit, and then surprisingly fell to his knees. She had not struck him that hard, but he fell over on his side. Out of the corner of her eye, she noticed an object flash. His knife! She had forgotten it and he was attempting to retrieve it.

"Oh, no, you will not!"

Stepping on his knuckles and whacking him with the shovel, she kicked the knife back towards the door.

He tried to grab her feet out from under her, but never let it be said that Hattie Longbottom, no Weston, she reminded herself, was not an agile dancer. She evaded his clutches while managing to spin around and plant the end of the shovel squarely in the back of his head. His eyes rolled backwards and blood began to pour from his head.

"Oh Lord, what have I done?"

Quickly, she was on her knees, trying to stem the flow of blood; frantically ripping at her new petticoats and holding pressure against the otherwise lifeless form.

"Please, God, let someone find us before he bleeds to death!" she sobbed.

Thou shalt not commit murder! The Reverend Hastings' voice, speaking the sixth commandment, played in her mind.

"Harriet Eleanor...Weston, you will hang and burn in hell for this!" She proceeded to torture herself thus for some time as she watched the horrid man dying in front of her very eyes.

"Murderer! Murderer!" she heard Archie crow outside as the rain eased, but unfortunately he was unable to open latches on shed doors and he had not gone for help as she had hoped. Her face fell in her hands in desperation.

CHAPTER 10

Edward debated the best way to engage Philip Martin. He believed, if he could get him talking, it would increase the possibility of the man incriminating himself. If Edward knew more about Martin, he could possibly know his vulnerabilities. He recalled the conversation Hattie had related. Apparently, the man loathed being threatened. That was interesting, he mused; it could be one approach to discovering the truth.

Bergen rode up beside him. "Weston, there is something more happening here with Hampton than accumulating simple gambling debts. Consider this, my friend. Compare the difference in your reaction to having a promissory note held over your head, to perhaps, a secret that could injure you. Hampton seems terrified of something or someone."

"Yes, you could be right." He thought about his brother. "Hampton was Edward's friend. I do not know what it is, but if I can get Martin to admit he did the killing, I will do whatever I can to stop his revelations."

"I concur—but how?"

"I am not sure. To be honest, I feel like we are stepping forward blindfolded, but that seems the only thing we can do. We do not have the luxury of planning. He is leaving." Edward looked behind him. Hampton was still trailing them by some distance. "He is still back there. There is no sign of bravado or enthusiasm—even with us by his side." In less than an hour, the trio arrived at the Bentley estate. The property was situated amongst several sloping areas. A large rose garden framed with boxwoods and a slight hill separated the home from a stone building housing the stables, giving the barn area a more distant feel. They made their way to the horse stalls.

"Will you wait here for me?" Edward spoke to Bergen, while he watched Hampton. "I will talk to the head groom and arrange a safe place for Hampton and the horses." He strode across the stable yard to the harness room, returning a few minutes later with a grizzled-haired horseman in tow. "The groom has offered us a stall in the far corner for our operation." He noticed Hampton was staring off in the distance. "Hampton?" Edward gained the man's attention, and pointed him to the end of the shadowy building. "The rearmost stall is yours. It has recently been mucked out."

Hampton scowled and then sneered, "I do not know what to say."

Edward gave his brother's friend a hard stare. "Hampton, tell us everything you feel we should know—*now*. Let us not let Martin have the element of surprise over us. I have known you almost your whole life. We grew up together, and I know the good man you are." He softened his petition. "I am your friend."

Hampton looked around. He started to speak, but closed his mouth before any words came forth, apparently changing his mind.

Edward turned at the sound of horses in the near distance, then quickly moved inside the door of the barn, out of sight, but still able to see the rider. A stocky balding man with a brown overcoat crested the hill. "The magistrate is coming over the rise. Bergen, you say you know this man?" Edward nodded behind them.

"Yes. He has an excellent arrest record in these parts. Very few escape his justice." He chuckled.

"One whom always gets his man. Excellent. It is a five-minute walk to the house. Let us get the note written." He produced a sheet of vellum and a pen from his saddlebags.

Bergen handed his horse to a waiting groom and ran up the steps to the front entrance. He tapped the brass knocker on the door. After a couple of minutes, he knocked again.

"Murderer! Help!" He heard the cry of a familiar bird.

Bergen banged the dark wooden door with his fists. A few moments later, an aged butler opened it. Before Bergen could speak, Archie flew from the shrub behind him, straight into the house. He landed in the hall, jumping from the banister of the staircase to the base of the glass transom above the door and back.

"Help! Murderer! Fly home Archie!" The bird leaped towards Bergen and slapped his face frantically with his wing. "Help! Help!"

"Archie, where is Lady Weston?"

"I am here. Who is looking for me?"

"My apologies, my lady. I am looking for your daughter-in-law. Archie seems to have misplaced her." He studied the bird for a moment. "It is strange, since I left him in his cage."

"Murderer! Help! Fly Archie!" The parrot hopped towards the door and began pecking at it frantically.

The Dowager's face went pale. "Archie, where is your mistress? How long has he been here?" She looked at Bergen.

"He arrived at the same time I did. Do you think this storm frightened him away from her ladyship?" Bergen held out his arm and the bird landed on it.

"My lord, you might be the only other person who could get him to do that." The Dowager nodded her approval. "My daughter-in-law took him to the orangery this afternoon. I left her there when I returned for my afternoon rest. It was before the heavy rain came. I have not seen her since. Yet, Archie is here. Could something have happened to her?"

"Why do you say that, my lady? Is there anything Lady Weston mentioned which makes you uneasy? I too, find Archie's presence disturbing."

"Help! Fly home! Help!" An agitated Archie flew off his arm and circled the area in front of the door.

"I think he wants us to follow him," Bergen said.

"Yes! I agree. Archie lead us to Hattie." The Dowager grabbed her cloak from the patiently waiting butler, and setting off outside together, the two of them did the best they could to encourage the bird to lead them.

⁓

"We have been here at the stables for twenty minutes. It is too quiet. Something is wrong." Edward spoke to the magistrate, Squire Sykes, who had arrived.

The portly man rubbed his chin before responding. I am inclined to agree. "From what you have explained of your plan, Lord Bergen should have been back by now, it seems. My lord, my mother always told me to listen to your inner self. It has saved my life on a number of occasions. If you think we should be somewhere else, let us proceed."

Edward called to the head groom. "Kindly inform Lord Hampton that our plan did not come together as we had hoped. Squire Sykes and I are heading towards the manor, with some urgency. Please ask him to join us there." With that, he nudged his mount into a canter and the two men sped across the park to the Bentley house.

As they reached the ridge of the hill, Edward saw the strangest sight. His mother was running behind Bergen, who was following his wife's large, colorful bird. A chill went up his spine. "Hattie is in trouble. Come! We must catch up to them."

"My lord, who is Hattie?"

"My wife." Edward spurred his horse, and within seconds the two men had caught up with Archie. Edward slowed down. "Mother, what are you doing out here running after Archie?"

"Your wife is without her bird, Edward. She had taken him to the orangery. I have not seen her since. Go! Find her!" She stopped and grabbed her waist, doubling over to catch her breath.

"My lady. Are you quite well?"

"Go, Bergen! I fear I am not accustomed to such exercise. I have just made friends with my daughter-in-law and I fear for her safety. Go and find her, sir!"

"Mother, please return to the house and get help." Edward and Sykes remained mounted, while Bergen remained on foot, all three chasing after the bird.

"Murderer! Fly Archie!" The popinjay headed towards the edge of the gardened area, with the three men following. They crossed the formal gardens and entered an enclosed garth where the gardener kept the nursery beds and his tools in a shed. Sounds of weeping could be heard as they approached the small building.

"Murderer! Murderer!" Archie crowed.

"Hattie!" Edward leaped off his horse. He tried the latch, but the door was stuck fast. Furiously, he pulled at it with his foot against the jam, in an effort to release it. The door swung open, slamming against the wall. Hattie sat next to a prone Philip Martin, holding a bloodied shovel in her hands.

"Hattie!" Pulling her to her feet, Edward held her against him. "What happened here?

"Is he alive, Edward?" She hiccuped. "He killed him. Mr. Martin murdered your brother and was going to kill Archie and me." She held up her tool. "I accidentally hit him, and I think he may be dead. There is so much blood!"

Bergen walked over to the man lying on the rough floor in front of him. He nudged him with his boot. Martin groaned and tried to sit up.

"I will kill you," Martin muttered as he raised his head and opened his eyes.

"You worthless piece of humanity," Edward growled. "You murdered my brother and let everyone think he died in a duel. Now you dare to threaten my wife..." Releasing Hattie, Edward strode forward, grabbed Martin by the collar and pulled him up, holding him at eye level. The man hung slack in his arms.

"Wait, Weston. I will take it from here." The magistrate pushed through to where Edward stood holding Martin. "My lady, I have no idea how you have accomplished this. You are a slight young woman. It is astonishing you were able to overpower this man on your own." He shook his head in disbelief. "I shall take him to the gaol, where he will await the assizes."

"I hope you hang for your misdeeds," the Dowager intoned as she arrived, still gasping for air, and faced her son's murderer.

Hampton made it to the shed just as the magistrate was ready to haul Philip Martin away.

Martin held up his head and sneered at Hampton. "You! I told you I would let the world know of your sorry existence."

"Go ahead. It will be your word, your lies, against my word." Hampton shook as he spoke. He turned to Edward. "I saw him shoot Robert. He threatened to kill me." He turned to the magistrate. "I will testify against him."

"As will I." Hattie brushed off her skirt. "He confessed to me."

"Liar! You will pay for this!" Martin continued belligerently.

Edward punched him in the mouth; Martin's body fell limp against Sykes. "You will keep your threats to yourself, sir!"

～

After the magistrate had taken statements from everyone and hauled Martin away to the gaol, they sat in the drawing room, conversing and attempting to replay the events for those who missed the excitement.

"I do believe Archie saved the day," Bergen mused as the parrot continued to show his preference for the man by sitting on his shoulder and rubbing his head against his neck.

"Indeed he did," the Dowager agreed. "Who knows how long it would have been before we found Hattie if it were not for Archie."

"Do you hear that, Archie? You are a hero!" Hattie exclaimed.

"Hero! Hero!" he mimicked to the laughter of all of those congregated, except for Louisa, Hattie noticed. She did wonder what was going through Louisa's mind after seeing her brother arrested for murder and whether or not her own sins would be exposed. Hattie decided she would leave it to her to tell or not. At least Richard was not implicated in the crimes—not that Hattie ever suspected as much.

"Oh!" Hattie exclaimed.

"What is it, dear?" Edward asked with concern.

"My new spectacles! They flew off during the struggle and in all of the fuss, I forgot to retrieve them." She stood frantically to go find them.

"We can send a footman for them now that the rain has stopped, Hattie," Richard suggested.

"But these were a very special gift," she said, worrying that these would have been crushed, too. "I think I know where they are."

"I will go with you." Edward rose and took her hand to accompany her.

"What a considerate husband he is," Hattie heard the Dowager remark proudly. There would be a better relationship for Edward and his mother going forward—she would make it her mission. They followed the path from the conservatory across the terrace and towards the lake as she had before, and began to search for the missing spectacles that symbolized everything she hoped for in a marriage: sight, thoughtfulness, kindness, and perhaps the promise of love. Edward bent down to retrieve the errant specs and, after he'd dried them off, slipped them back onto her face with a tender peck on the nose. They were unbroken, much to her relief.

"Now that the mystery is solved, where would you like to take a wedding trip?" Edward asked as they strolled hand in hand.

"It is not necessary to do such a thing, my Lord," Hattie replied meekly.

"But it is, dear wife. We need a fresh start away from our well-intentioned family."

"And some not-so-well-intentioned," she added dryly.

"Just so. Is there nowhere you have longed to visit?"

"Well," she wrinkled her brow with thought. "I have never been to London."

"London will be one of our homes. Anywhere else? Paris? Venice?"

"I could not leave Archie for so long!"

"He enjoys Bergen's company." His eyes twinkled down at her mischievously.

She thwacked his arm. "Do be serious, my lord."

"We might have started off on the wrong foot, and neither of us might have chosen the other, but Fate chose us. And I would very much like to have a good marriage."

"As would I. You are not at all what I judged you to be when I first saw you."

"Nor are you, thank the Lord above."

She angled an eyebrow at him for his use of the Lord's name.

"We seem to have started properly in one area," he looked at her from beneath hooded eyelids—the way he had looked at her in their bedroom after their first union. A warm tingle began to spread through her body to her womb. She was coming to recognize the signs of desire. He must have noticed the change in her—wanton behavior indeed! No wonder young ladies were kept under strict chaperonage until marriage.

"What *did* you expect?" Hattie managed to ask.

"I am sure I should not answer that. I will say I am most pleased with you." Edward stepped closer to her with a predatory look in his eye.

"We are expected for dinner," she said unconvincingly, as her voice cracked with pleasure.

"I certainly am hungry," he said as he took a taste of her neck with his tongue. Her entire body shivered in response. Rational thoughts fluttered out the window.

"I suddenly am not," she whispered breathlessly as he began to unhook her bodice.

"I did not mean for food, dear wife," he said with a wicked glance up at her while bringing pleasure to one of her breasts.

Hattie's knees weakened. "But will they not come looking for us if we are absent?"

"I am fairly certain they will understand."

She shrieked as he drew her behind a neatly maintained row of yew trees and divested her of the remains of her clothing, and then proceeded to divest himself of his.

"But they will know what we are doing!"

"Hattie?"

"Yes?"

"We are husband and wife, ordained by Holy Matrimony. Stop thinking. Stop talking. Make love to me."

He continued his machinations doing deliciously naughty things to her body.

Perhaps marrying a wicked earl was not the worst thing that could have happened to her, she reflected. Then he entered her and shocks of pleasure waved through her body.

No, Hattie never would have chosen a rake or a rogue for her lawfully wedded husband, but she did believe in Divine Intervention, and who was she to argue?

PREVIEW EARL OF DAVENPORT

BY MAGGIE DALLEN

The sound of a carriage coming up the drive had Anne and her chaperone hurrying toward the drawing room window in a manner that was entirely unbecoming for two proper young ladies. Although, it seemed to Anne that being late to one's scheduled meeting with two proper young ladies was equally unbecoming, so perhaps it could be overlooked.

Her chaperone, Betsy, went so far as to peek through the curtains, while Anne contented herself by leaning a tad to the left so she could see through one of the cracks where the curtain fell away from the wall.

"Here comes the devil himself," Betsy murmured.

Typically, Anne would have scolded her former governess for the breach in etiquette. The man was an earl, for heaven's sake, he should be referred to by his title. But she kept her mouth shut. The entire country knew him as the Devil of Davenport. Scolding Betsy wouldn't change that.

Besides, Betsy didn't know the earl the way that Anne did. As far as Anne was aware, she was the only one who knew Davenport's well-kept secret.

He wasn't a devil, not really. Not at all.

PREVIEW EARL OF DAVENPORT

In fact, he was every bit a gentleman.

She watched the gentleman in question stride into the house with a few muffled orders to the footman who'd met him at the carriage door. Anne could only wonder if he would make them wait much longer.

Now that he was here, the butterflies in her stomach went into a flurry of activity. Drawing a deep breath, she reached for the back of a nearby chair to try and calm her nerves.

There was no need to be nervous. This was Davenport, not some beastly rake as the scandal sheets would have one believe. As the owner of the land neighboring her family's, she'd known him since forever, it seemed. If anyone could help them, it was him. And surely he would help. He had to.

He was their last hope.

"I cannot imagine what you were thinking coming here this morning, Anne," Betsy said, interrupting her thoughts, her voice filled with disapproval.

Anne bit back a sigh. Her friend was not helping to fortify her courage.

"You have done a great deal of silly things in your day, miss, but this is the most ludicrous of them all."

Anne pressed her lips together and stared with determination at the door where he would enter. She should not have brought Betsy. She wished she hadn't. But of course, she'd had to. Who else would have come? As a young, unmarried woman it would be unseemly to visit *any* gentleman alone, but to visit the so-called devil himself?

That kind of ruination could never be undone.

Anne might not have had much of a reputation in society to begin with, thanks to the rumors about her family, but she refused to provide additional fodder for the gossips. "Betsy, do try to understand —" Her plea was interrupted when the door to the hallway swung open with undo force.

Anne's breath left her in a *whoosh*, the way it always did upon seeing him. No one could deny that Frederick William Belford, the Earl of Davenport, was a striking man. And now, standing here in the doorway—posing, really, as he leaned against the doorframe and openly assessed his visitors—Anne decided that *striking* didn't begin to describe him.

He was beautiful.

No, perhaps *beautiful* wasn't quite right either. That sounded far too feminine and delicate. And *handsome* seemed far too mundane. Definitely not *pretty*, that did not describe him at all. His features were too sharp for that, his shoulders too broad.

But he had an air about him that reminded her of one of the Arabian stallions her brother, Jed, liked to race. All sleek lines and barely restrained power. He moved with an easy grace and his strong jaw and firm mouth seemed to always be set in a way that spoke of strength and power.

There was an elegance about him, despite the fact that he didn't seem to heed the latest trends. Like now, for instance. His black hair was just a tad too long and the jaw she so admired was clearly in need of a shave. Despite his haughty expression, his clothes were ruffled and mussed. Almost like he'd slept in them, or....

Her throat grew dry as it became very clear why he was late to an early morning appointment at his own home.

He hadn't slept there.

The earl was just now arriving home, and it appeared he was wearing yesterday's clothes. By the smug look on his face, he didn't seem to care who knew. In fact, his smirk made her think he enjoyed the discomfort it caused.

Cheeky devil. No, not devil. She refused to use that awful nickname even in her thoughts. But just because she knew he was not the heathen the *ton* claimed him to be, that didn't mean he was a saint, either.

The Earl of Davenport was merely a man.

She licked her lips and took a steadying breath as she repeated that to herself. *He was merely a man.* But then he shifted and his shirt strained across the hard muscles of his chest, his breeches molding to his thighs as he moved. She tried to swallow. He was a man all right, but there was no *merely* about it.

His eyes moved over her just as studiously as she'd eyed him, but what he found did not seem to leave an impression. His gaze roamed over her bright red hair, her pale gray morning gown, all the way down to her slippers. She stood there stoically, as if awaiting some sort of judgement. But when his eyes met hers, there was nothing there. No verdict, no emotion... and no sign of recognition.

"Ah, my morning visitors," he said as he pushed himself away from the doorway and entered the room. His pace was slow and his tone held more than a hint of mockery. "How could I have forgotten the urgent summons from Miss...."

He reached the settee and fell onto it, his questioning gaze once more returning to Anne. Her eyes narrowed on him. What was he about? Of course he knew who she was. He was acting obtuse just to be a boor. Why he insisted on acting like a fiend when she clearly knew the truth about him, she would never understand.

"Miss Anne Cleveland," she finished. "And this is my dear friend, Mrs. Elizabeth Bawdry."

She'd very nearly pointed out that he knew exactly who she was—her family had been living on the property adjacent to his their entire lives, but she refrained on Betsy's account. The woman had suffered enough by coming along with her this morning. Despite her protests, Betsy was being a good sport. So, rather than risk being rude and causing Betsy more discomfort, she'd answered the unspoken question politely.

Davenport gave her friend a peremptory nod before turning back to her. His arm was slung over the back of the settee as he lounged there, looking for all the world like a sultan with his harem.

Her heart thumped erratically. Now where had that thought come from? Her admittedly overactive imagination hurried to provide her with an image to accompany the wayward thought. A shirtless Davenport lounging on a bed of pillows. Those dark gray eyes watching her as she undressed for him....

His low voice cut into the errant daydream. "Miss Cleveland, I find myself extraordinarily curious to know where your thoughts have gone."

She started, her mouth falling open in an unladylike manner as heat bloomed in her cheeks. Sweet heavens, she had been caught ogling the man.

He tilted his head to the side as he stared up at her. "You have remarkably expressive features, has anyone ever told you that?"

She shook her head. "No, my lord." *Blast.* That was a lie. Everyone had told her that. She was one of seven siblings and each and every one had commented on multiple occasions on their ability to read her like a book.

From the way he was smirking, she had the horrible sensation that he'd seen exactly where her mind had wandered. But then, he must have been used to women eyeing him like that. She rarely attended society events but she knew from her sister, Claire, that he was considered quite the catch.

He'd developed a reputation for his reckless behavior but that only seemed to enhance his appeal among the young ladies, and even their mamas overlooked his bad deeds on behalf of his title. Mothers looking to wed their daughters were capable of overlooking any number of things when it came to wealthy, titled gentlemen.

This line of thought brought her back to her senses. That was exactly why she was here. Because of good marriages and overbearing mamas, but most importantly, because of Claire.

Steeling her spine, she turned to Betsy. "Mrs. Bawdry, I do believe I've left my shawl with the butler and I seem to have developed a chill. Would you be so kind as to fetch it for me?"

The only sound was the ticking of the grandfather clock as Betsy glared at her, her eyes attempting to convey every lecture she'd already given a hundred times over. Anne met her stare with raised brows. They'd been over this and over this. She understood Betsy's objections, but this was the only way. She needed to speak with the earl and the conversation had to be done in private.

It would be difficult enough to get through to the man by herself but if he suspected he had an audience to impress with his ridiculous devil façade, her plight would not stand a chance.

After several long moments, Betsy conceded, but not without a

PREVIEW EARL OF DAVENPORT

grumble of warning before she headed back out the way they had come in. The door closed behind her with a click.

They were alone.

She was alone with the Devil of Davenport.

Shaking her head slightly, she turned back to face the man who was *not* a devil. His look of amusement had her blushing all over again.

"I must confess, I'm intrigued," he said, his voice a low rumble in the otherwise silent room. "Why would a proper young lady like yourself wish to be left unchaperoned with the likes of me?"

He came to a stand and once again, Anne was reminded of a beast. But not the black stallion in her brother's stables. This time he struck her as a predator. As he moved toward her, she backed away. It wasn't until the back of her legs hit an end table that she came to a stop.

She thought he would stop too, but he kept advancing until he was standing just in front of her, so close she could feel the heat radiating from his skin. The scent of soap and leather filled her senses and she clasped her hands together, partly to keep them from shaking with nerves, but partly because she had the ridiculous desire to reach out and touch him. He was so close that she could lift her hand and he would be there, his warm skin under her glove, his hard muscles pressed against her.

She shivered as a foreign sensation swept over her body, leaving her feeling exposed and vulnerable.

"Yes," he murmured softly. "I do wish I could read that mind of yours, Miss Cleveland. Though I'm not entirely sure I need to."

She forced herself to lift her gaze to meet his. *Oh mercy.* She wished she could look away from those eyes, darkened with an emotion so primal, she recognized it deep in her bones. *Desire.*

"I-I need to speak with you, my lord." Her voice had grown ridiculously breathy but she was proud that she had at least managed to get the words out.

He took one step back as some of the intensity eased from his demeanor and a smile hovered over his lips. "I gathered that from

PREVIEW EARL OF DAVENPORT

your missive." He turned his back on her to walk over to the settee once more and she found herself once again able to breathe.

"So tell me, Miss Cleveland. What can I do for you today?"

She took two long, deep breaths to steady her nerves before responding. "You see, my lord, you are in need of a wife."

His eyes widened with surprise before his head fell back with a short, harsh laugh. He lifted his head to face her. "I see. And that is why you are here." He leaned forward on the seat so his elbows were resting on his knees. "And tell me, are you offering yourself up for the role of countess?"

Her cheeks burned with humiliation. She'd gone about this all wrong. She'd rehearsed her speech for hours in the mirror yet she'd been too flustered to get it out in the proper order. Shaking her head, she whispered quickly, "Of course not, don't be silly."

Everyone knew she was not wife material—not for a gentleman, at least, and certainly not for an earl. She had been raised as one of the Cleveland children, but it was widely known, though never confirmed, that the Clevelands fell into two categories—the legitimate and the illegitimate. Their father had been kind enough to give them all his name and his wife had raised them as though they were her own, but none of that mattered to the *ton*. Aside from the eldest three, whose lineage had never been in question, the rest were the subject of gossip and scorn. There were questions about Roger and Delia, the middle two—no one knew for certain whether they were legitimate. She and her brother Caleb, however, were in a category all their own thanks to their blazing red hair. Everyone knew who their mother was. Apparently Kitty Furlong had been quite a star on the London stage at the time their father took up with her. Kitty was known for three things: her extravagant tastes, her notorious affairs, and her bright red hair.

The red hair left no doubt in anyone's minds about who her real mother was. So, despite the Cleveland name and the fact that no one could disprove her parents' claim that she was legitimate, she would never truly be considered a lady.

Which was fine by her. She'd become accustomed to her lot many years ago when her eldest sister Claire—one of the legitimate siblings —had explained to her kindly and gently why Anne was so often slighted by their peers. Since then, she'd come to embrace her life away from the watchful eyes of society. Though hardly enviable, her disreputable position came with a certain amount of freedom. Claire, on the other hand, had all the benefits of a good reputation as well as the name and the breeding.

Claire was the reason she was here, and that thought kept her going despite the nearly overwhelming flood of embarrassment. "As I see it, you are in need of a wife."

She winced slightly as her second attempt came out just as ineloquent as the first. Judging by his narrowed eyes and the mocking glint in his eyes, she'd do best to return home and start all over again on another day. Preferably many years from now when he'd long forgotten this bungled mess of a meeting.

Clearing her throat, she tried to put her thoughts in order, firmly ignoring his all-seeing gaze and those dark eyes that had always fascinated her. This was absolutely not the time to be admiring his finer qualities, not if she were to make it through this interview with any sort of success.

"What I mean to say," she said slowly, taking her time to find the right words on this next attempt, "is that it is no secret that you are looking for a wife."

He didn't argue and she hurried on before he could. She had no way of truly knowing about his matrimonial intentions, of course, but she heard enough gossip to know that he was in need of a countess. And an heir. Preferably one before the other, she'd imagine.

His estate did not require the money from a dowry and he was powerful enough to that he did not need another title, which was one more reason why this could be just the match Claire needed. No, by all accounts, what Davenport required was a wife. A proper wife who could give him an heir and help to restore his reputation.

She clasped her hands together as she made her proposition. "You see, my lord, I believe that my eldest sister, Claire Cleveland, would be the ideal candidate."

PREVIEW EARL OF DAVENPORT

His eyes widened slightly but that was the only reaction. She assumed that was her cue to continue.

"I know it is very forward of me to come here like this, but—"

"But what, Miss Cleveland?"

She stilled. Oh sweet mercy, his voice was a menacing growl, at odds with his casual demeanor as he leaned back in his chair.

Terror struck, making her shiver. Perhaps she'd overstepped her bounds. Maybe Betsy had been right and she was making a fool of herself in front of an earl, of all people.

But as quickly as terror came, it abated. Reason stepped in as soon as she drew her next breath. This wasn't just some member of the gentry. Davenport was far from the typical earl, and that was precisely why she was here.

She knew what no one else did. Much as he pretended to be a devil, he'd always been her savior. Her personal champion. The boy she'd adored from afar growing up, and now the man who she was certain would help her and her family.

Still, even knowing that didn't help to dispel the nerves that had her clasping her hands together for courage. "I know that despite the rakish persona you've adopted, you are a good man."

His lips twisted in a mocking grin that made her tremble. She refused to let that stop her from speaking the truth. "You have always been kind to my family, and it is that kindness that I am appealing to now."

She felt his hesitation, almost as though his instinctual mockery and disbelief were tempered by curiosity. Maybe even concern. She let herself be buoyed by that hopeful thought. "You see, my lord, my family is in dire straits. We are on the verge of losing everything and most of my siblings have given up any chance of saving our home or our land, but—"

He finally interjected, his voice droll and his eyes revealing nothing. "But you think that I could swoop in and save you. Your entire family. The whole incongruous lot of you."

She felt blood rushing to her cheeks at the scorn in his voice. Anne was used to hearing derision when it came to her family, particularly her and her younger siblings. But to hear it from him—from the man who had shielded her from the *ton's* mockery years ago. From the kind neighbor who she'd always thought of as friend, in an odd sort of way.

It hurt more than she cared to let on.

So instead, she did what she'd always done when her family was the subject of derision. She lifted her chin with pride. She might not be able to defend her father's actions or her eldest brother's, but there was at least one member of her family who was above reproach. "My eldest sister, Claire, is the perfect lady, she—"

"Which one is Claire?" he interrupted.

Her eyes narrowed and her nostrils flared as a surge of annoyance swept over her, and this time she failed to contain it. "You know very well who she is," she snapped.

His brows shot up and his eyes filled with laughter as he stood and walked toward her. "Ah, there she is. I'd been wondering who this meek, demure young lady in my drawing room was, but now I recognize you clearly, my little hellion."

Her cheeks warmed again, but this time with something close to pleasure. So he did remember. He'd been teasing her, after all. Little hellion was what he'd called her when she was young and chased after him and her eldest brother. He and Jed had terrorized the villagers with their pranks and hijinks and she'd done her very best to tag along.

She cleared her throat. "Yes, my lord. The little hellion is in your midst, I'm afraid."

His lips tilted up in a grin that made her heart race.

"If you remember me, then surely you must remember Claire. She's the eldest daughter, and the loveliest by far."

"Says who?" he interrupted.

"Excuse me?"

"What powerful deity declared Claire the fairest Cleveland of them all?"

She scowled at his teasing and carried on. "As I was saying, not only is she lovely, but she is the perfect lady. Genteel and polished, she is beloved by the *ton*."

PREVIEW EARL OF DAVENPORT

He gave an exaggerated yawn.

When she blinked up at him, he waved a hand for her to continue. "Do go on. Genteel, polished, etcetera, etcetera…."

He was mocking her. As he walked away she squelched the urge to stomp her foot to regain his attention. She settled for letting out an exhale that was louder than necessary. Then, when he still did not turn around, she blurted out her request. "I'd like you to consider Claire for a wife, my lord."

That made him turn around to face her, at least, though his expression was one of droll amusement.

She hated that look—it reeked of condescension and entitlement. She was used to seeing that expression on the faces of the *ton*, but she expected more from this man.

Which was ironic, really, since the rest of society expected so little of him.

"Tell me, little hellion, are you really asking me to marry your sister as an act of charity?"

Her eyes widened and her hands clenched at her side. It was through gritted teeth that she finally managed to answer. "Not at all, my lord. Any man would be lucky to have Claire as his bride."

His smirk had her taking deep breaths to remain calm. Lord, he could be infuriating when he wanted to be. "Yes, it would benefit my family as well," she conceded, "But just think what this marriage could do for you."

He fell back onto the settee once more, looking as though his patience was reaching an end. "And what exactly would Claire provide for me that all the other demure, genteel debutantes could not?"

"Honesty, respectability—"

His brows arched. "You cannot be serious. Respectability from the Clevelands?"

She rose to her full height, tilting her chin up once more. "Say what you will about me, but Claire is as respectable as they come."

"And by that you mean, there's no suspicion that she's a bastard."

His words were spoken so casually it made their impact that much more dramatic.

She gaped at him, speechless. No one used that word around her. She was certain it was used behind their backs regularly, but no one had the gall to say it to her face. For a moment she was offended, then horrified, and then... amused.

She slapped a hand over her mouth to stifle an entirely inappropriate laugh, emitting a rather unladylike choking noise instead.

His eyes laughed at her, those dark gray eyes filled with knowing amusement.

She sobered instantly. It had been shock, that was all. And perhaps just a bit of relief that for once someone in society said what they meant. After a lifetime of being spoken about in whispers, it was almost refreshing to hear the insult aloud and to one's face.

He'd been hoping to shock her, that much was clear. Looking at him now, it was also clear there was only one way to proceed, and that was to be as honest as he was being now.

"That is correct, my lord," she said, casting her eyes downward. "Unlike myself and the other younger Clevelands, there is no tarnish on Claire's name."

His lips turned up in genuine amusement and he leaned back further in his seat. She got the distinct impression that he was pleased by her candor.

Well, if he wanted candor he would get it. "Claire is well known for her even temper and generosity. She has the education and upbringing to make her an exceptional countess."

He didn't look impressed.

She took a deep breath. She'd come this far, there was no turning back. "You must know what they say about you, my lord—"

"Enough with the formalities," he said, waving his hand as if brushing them aside. "If you're going to lecture me on my poor reputation, you might as well refer to me by my name."

She straightened her spine, refusing to drop her gaze despite the open mockery in his eyes. "Very well. You must know what they say about you, Davenport."

PREVIEW EARL OF DAVENPORT

His lips turned up on one side. "Better." He leaned forward. "Tell me, what is it they say?"

He was trying to fluster her further, but it would not work. If he could use the word bastard to her face, surely she could muster up the courage to call him by his nickname. "They call you devil, my lor—er, Davenport."

"Do they now?"

She scowled at his teasing tone. "More than that, they say that you're losing the confidence of your tenants and that your lands and properties are suffering from a lack of guidance."

He opened his mouth but she kept talking before he could throw out another amused barb. "You might not want a wife, my lord, but it certainly seems as though you need one."

His brows shot up at that, and behind the mockery she thought she sensed a new interest. Encouraged by the shift in him, she hurried on. "Whatever they might say about you, I believe that you'd do what's best. For your tenants and…." She swallowed down emotions that threatened to choke her. "And for your neighbors."

His eyes moved over her face, down her throat and to the edge of her bodice. She grasped her skirts to keep her hands from fluttering up to self-consciously hide herself from his gaze. She was dressed perfectly modestly, she had nothing to hide.

So why did she feel so exposed?

His silence lasted so long that she started to wonder if perhaps he was waiting on her. "Would you like to hear more about my sister, my lord?" she offered tentatively.

His brows drew together. "Good God, no. And what happened to you using my name?"

She bit her lip to keep from pestering him. It didn't work. "Well?" she asked, desperation overcoming any hope she had to leave here with her dignity intact. "What do you think?"

He let out a laugh—an honest to goodness laugh, not one filled with mockery or cynicism. "Impatient, are we?"

She nodded. There was no use denying it. For a moment she thought about telling him the extent of their bad fortune. Explaining

PREVIEW EARL OF DAVENPORT

to him that they were mere moments away from losing everything. But something held her back. There was a line, she supposed, that separated concern from pity and she was loathe to see the latter in his eyes.

Another few seconds passed and she was certain that he would never answer. Finally, however, he stood from the settee and headed toward the door. As he left, she heard him call out, "I'll think about it."

ACKNOWLEDGMENTS

Thank you' to a very special friend who believed in me and said, "Let's try this!" And from that...Archie, Edward and Hattie became our first book!

Anna St. Claire

ABOUT THE AUTHOR

Anna St. Claire is an avid reader, and now author, of both American and British historical romance. She and her husband live in Charlotte, North Carolina, where their once empty nest has filled with her cat, two dogs, and her new granddaughter.

Anna relocated from New York to the Carolinas as a child. Her mother, a retired English and History teacher, always encouraged Anna's interest in writing, after discovering short stories she would write in her spare time.

Her fascination with history and reading led her to her first historical romance—Margaret Mitchell's *Gone With The Wind*. The day she discovered Kathleen Woodiwiss,' books, *Shanna* and *Ashes In The Wind*, Anna was hooked. She read every historical romance that came her way. Today, her focus is primarily the Civil War and Regency eras, although Anna enjoys almost any period in American and British history.

She would love to connect with any of her readers at annastclaireauthor@gmail.com.

Printed in Great Britain
by Amazon